9780425031476
AF572135

The Gray Death

It struck the proudest ship of Patanga's fleet, and left its picked crew dead or howling in their madness. And swift on the heels of this horror came news that a renegade wizard and a pirate king were moving against Patanga, armed with mastery of the invincible Gray Death!

Patanga's warrior-king, Thongor the mighty, set out on a desperate mission to counter the deadly sorcery that doomed his realm...and vanished from the sight of men!

This is the third in the new series of the exploits of Thongor, mightiest warrior of the storied continent of Lemuria.

By the Same Author

THONGOR AND THE WIZARD OF LEMURIA

Thongor Fights The Pirates Of Tarakus

Lin Carter

A BERKLEY MEDALLION BOOK
published by
BERKLEY PUBLISHING CORPORATION

THONGOR FIGHTS THE PIRATES OF TARAKUS
is dedicated to three of Thongor's most devoted fans,

AUDREY TINSLEY,
CARTER LUPTON,
and DREW SMITH,

who are thus created *kojans* of the Empire
with all best wishes of their friend, Lin Carter

Copyright © 1970, by Lin Carter

All rights reserved

Published by arrangement with the author's agent.

All rights reserved which includes the right to reproduce this book or portions thereof in any form whatsoever. For information address

Henry Morrison, Inc.
58 West 10th Street
New York, N. Y.

SBN 425-03147-0

BERKLEY MEDALLION BOOKS are published by
Berkley Publishing Corporation
200 Madison Avenue
New York, N. Y. 10016

BERKLEY MEDALLION BOOK ® TM 757,375

Printed in the United States of America

Berkley Medallion Edition, JUNE, 1976

SECOND PRINTING

Author's Note

According to the occultists, the first civilizations of man upon this planet came into being half a million years ago on the Lost Continent of Lemuria in the blue Pacific.

Of these kingdoms of the dawn—now long since forgotten and but vaguely whispered of in scraps of elder legend and ancient myth—the mightiest was The Golden Empire of the Sun. To the Lemurians themselves it was the *Shamgamma*, the Great Union. Although I have translated the term as "empire" it actually bore very little resemblance to the general meaning of that word. It seems to have been a league of free cities which acknowledged the King of Patanga as their Overlord. (Incidentally, some authorities believe the ancient Lemurian language was among the ancestors of early Sanskrit. This may or may not be true, but there exists an interesting parallel between the Lemurian word *Shamgamma*, Great Union, and the old Sanskrit *samgam*, which means monad or unity.)

According to such prehistoric legendary Indian epics as the Puranas, this Golden Empire of the Sun was founded by a wandering barbarian adventurer whom I have called Thongor. I have recorded a history of his adventures in a series of fantastic novels of which *Thongor Fights the Pirates of Tarakus* is the sixth.

This book takes place three years after the events narrated in *Thongor at the End of Time*, in the late fall of the Year of the Kingdoms of Man seven-thousand-and-twenty.

—LIN CARTER

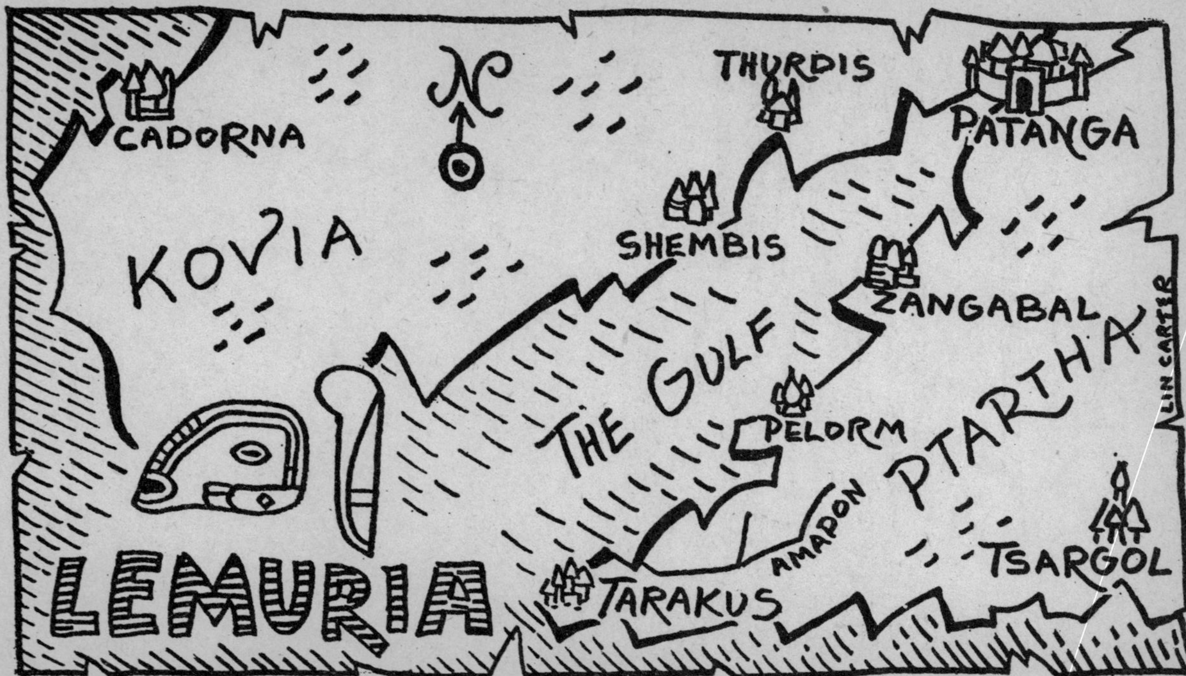
CADORNA
N
THURDIS
PATANGA
KOVIA
SHEMBIS
ZANGABAL
THE GULF
PELORM
PTARTHA
LIN CARTER
AMADON
TSARGOL
TARAKUS
LEMURIA

BOOK ONE

THE STORM GATHERS

"Below the Gulf of Patanga, aye, where it mingles with the immeasurable waters of Yashengzeb Chun the Southern Sea, there stands a great promontory of rock whereon is builded Tarakus the Pirate City, a lawless and bloody realm that knoweth no rule save the lust of gold. Therefrom, in the long years ahead, a peril shall rise up to enshadow the Cities of the West, so beware, O Thongor . . . take warning and beware."

—*The Great Book of Sharajsha the Wizard*

CHAPTER 1:

THE SHIP OF HOWLING MEN

A strange dark ship, at the death of day,
With a crew of howling men,
Who had looked on hell and come away,
But were no longer men . . .

—The Tsargol Records

IT was the month of Zorah, the third month of fall, in the twelfth year of the reign of Thongor the Mighty over the Six Cities, when a ship came slowly into the harbor of Tsargol at sundown.

Night was almost come and the sun lay dying in a welter of crimson athwart the shadowy west. Slowly the purple wings of night rose up over the edges of the earth to enshroud the world in darkness. The first stars flickered pale and dim against the dusk. Soon Illana the Moon-Lady would ascend the heavens to flood all the land with her cold shimmering glory, but not yet, for still bright Aedir the Sun-god ruled the skies from his deathbed of royal crimson in the darkling west.

The red stone city of Tsargol rose on the wave-lashed shores of the southern Sea. Tall towers and stout walls guarded it from assault; proud palaces and stately temples displayed the wealth and power of the City of the Sea; its populace enjoyed the mild autumn evening on terraces and in luxurious gardens, and strolled at leisure along the broad stone-paved avenues.

The ship crept into the harbor and at first few saw it for no lamps twinkled at mast-head or prow. The mighty trireme was a moving shape of shadows as it glided slowly through the dark waters. It passed the mole and came within the mighty sea wall that encircled the man-made harbor in sheltering arms of stone. Then it was that a keen-eyed watchman high on the walls of Tsargol spied the slowly moving ship and gave the alarm.

Gongs roared. Torches flared. Spearmen seized up

burning brands and went pelting down the spray-wet stone steps to the sea wall to learn what mariner dared enter the harbor of Tsargol without lamps burning or flags aloft.

The huge trireme slowly crossed the harbor. Watchful eyes traced its passage and strong hands tightened on spear and bow and swordhilt. Otars in command of a hundred warriors passed grim orders to waiting messengers. A herald sprang astride a kroter and drove his knees into the scaly ribs of the swift-footed reptile and rode clattering off to the palace of Karm Karvus, Lord of the City.

It was not surprising that the unexpected appearance of one ship should cause such consternation and alarm, for these were the southern coasts and all these lands went in dread of the bold and rapacious corsairs of Tarakus the Pirate City. No ship was safe on these buccaneer-infested waters and no port could feel fully secure. That lone trireme might well be the advance scout of the terrible armada of Tarakus. In its wake a hundred slim black hulls might cruise, swarming with bloody pirates eager to rape the wealth of fabulous Tsargol.

At length it was perceived that the intruder was unaccompanied. And sharp eyes soon guessed the mighty trireme was in trouble. For her triple oarbanks were largely unoccupied and the swinging stroke of oars dipped in unison—which should have driven the great ship forward with a smooth, gliding progress—moved instead to a broken rhythm. The oars were plied by few hands, and awkwardly. She moved slowly, crabwise, and at times her prow skewed about and she wallowed against the waves.

Soon other eyes noted that her sails were torn and partly furled, but bound up all wrong and crudely. As she drew nearer to the long stone quays that thrust out from the inner crescent of the harbor, it was observed that her rail was smashed and broken, gilded wood crushed and torn away, and that the mighty dragon's head of her prow was broken and shoved askew.

And as she came nearer to the quays, a faint horrible sound came to the ears of the Guardsmen who stood waiting to board her. It was a hideous ululation. It rose and fell, a moaning terrible and unnerving to hear. Otar looked at Otar with eyes wide with horror. The men of the dark, crippled ship were . . . *howling* . . .

Then one young officer saw with a sudden thrill of alarm that the oars were not back-sweeping to ease the trireme into her berth, but, instead, still swept her forward in that crippled, arhythmic progress. He raised a shout of alarm.

"Board ship—'ware the quay! *Back water,* you fools, before you hit the—"

His sudden shout was drowned in a mighty grinding and buckling of timbers as the strange ship drove full against the side of the stone dock. The impact made the granite quay shudder underfoot. The ship lurched—skewed drunkenly—and came to a dead halt. One sail came crashing down and the mast creaked alarmingly, and splintered with a deafening screech of tearing oak. Then all was still.

But the men howled on. A mournful, hellish chorus like the groans of the damned, whimpering and mewling under the torments of demons.

Among the spearsmen, men cursed and paled and gripped their weapons tighter, knuckles whitening from the strain. Was the strange dark ship peopled by madmen? Or had it drifted into human seas from the crimson throat of hell itself, manned by the accursed? Were they madmen—or ghosts—aboard the weird craft that had come out of the unknown watery wastes in the hour of sunfall?

Hooves clattered against the cobbles, and Karim Ptole the Commander of the Port came into view, gold helm glittering in the streaming torchlight.

"Ho, there, Otar! Secure the trireme and get your men aboard. You, there! Get a rope around her prow before she grinds half her hull to splinters against the quay! Swiftly, you men!"

A grizzled Daotar, commander of ten companies, strode to where the Commander sat astride his pacing kroter. The gray-bearded officer saluted stiffly with one balled fist against his heart.

"What think you?" growled Karim Ptole harshly. "Plague—or piracy?"

The Daotar squinted in the flickering torchfire, as warriors made the trireme secure with tossed grapnels, roped her to the piles, and swarmed aboard, swords ready. He grunted and spat.

"The sea wolves of Tarakus sink their prey," he observed grimly. "Seldom do men escape their clutches once the crimson flag is hoisted aloft and the black hulls glide in for the kill. In truth, Lord, I know not what to make of this . . . mayhap a sea monster attacked the trireme and savaged what it could not eat?"

"Perchance," Karim Ptole growled. "But . . . there is something devilishly familiar about that craft, the lines of her, the curve of her prow . . . almost I could swear I had laid my eyes on her before . . ."

"Well, perchance you have, Lord," the old Daotar mused. "I, too, feel I have known the lines of her . . . that brightwork on the afterdeck, those carven and gilded dolphins sporting along her rail in a running frieze . . ."

His pale eyes narrowed thoughtfully.

"Yet she's no naval craft, that's for sure, and no merchantman either, with that keel. Some princeling's royal yacht? Some fat admiral's pleasure-ship, mayhap?"

The mounted Commander shook his head, helm glittering.

"Almost she reminds me of the *Crown of Tsargol* herself," he muttered. "But Prince Karm Karvus, our lord and master, took her to sea three days ago for a visit-of-state to Vozashpa, so it could not be—"

He broke off and his face went pale under his bronze tan. At the same instant, the Daotar who stood at his stirrup, squinting through the gathering darkness at the mauled and splintered prow stifled a sharp cry of horror as he made out the glyphs of the trireme's name written in gold thereupon.

The Crown of Tsargol . . .

*

THE young Otar, Jorn Javas, was the first aboard the mystery ship. He sprang up and seized one of the ropes and swung up and over the rail and down into the oarbanks. He stopped short at what he saw, with a gasp of astonishment and horror.

Corpses were strewn about the benches. Their gore smeared the broken oars and besplattered the decks. They had not died easily.

He peered closer, striving to make out elusive details through the gloom. He reached down and turned one body over.

The tanned and bearded face of a sailor stared up at him, eyes wide and glaring and awful. Soapy foam smeared the dead man's lips, which were drawn back in a frozen rictus, half snarl and half grin. The man's throat had been cut from ear to ear. *And the dirk that had done the deed was clenched in the man's own hand.*

His face grim and set, Jorn Javas prowled the benches, examining the dead. Some had died at their own hands, but others had died locked in battle with their own comrades. He turned shuddering away from one ghastly sight: two mariners still tangled in each others' arms, their teeth sunk deep in each other's throats . . .

But not all were dead. Some there were who yet lived. And the sight of them was more terrible than the sight of the mangled dead.

They sat idly, hands on their oars, and peered at him strangely when he spoke to them. Some wept; others laughed wildly. Jorn Javas went from man to man, gazing into blood-smeared faces, glazed and vacant eyes, mouths that drooled and slobbered. He knew that they were mad. From the mindless men at the oars a moaning sound rose and fell, rose and fell, from a mournful sobbing to a howling like the baying of tormented animals.

Though young, Jorn Javas was no white-fingered recruit but a seasoned veteran. He had slain men in his time, and he had looked on the ugly visage of war and siege and assault. Dead men he had seen and not a few of them: men mangled by the engines of war and men gruesomely mauled by torture. None of those grim sights had moved him so terribly as did the nightmare decks of this dark ship from hell.

White faced, he turned and was sick, rackingly, horribly sick. Then he roused himself and continued his search of the ship.

The decks were strewn with bloody bodies, with dead men and with mewling, sobbing madmen. In their mindless fury they had wreaked great damage to the ship, which was accoutered for the pleasures of some mighty prince. Jorn Javas found smashed doors and torn brocades and silken hangings befouled with human offal. Bodies were tossed about, huddled in corners, spread-eagled on floors, hunched over bundles of rigging.

One man, at least, had resisted madness to the end.

It was the captain of the vessel, from his great crimson coat and gold brocade. A seasoned and experienced mariner, from the looks of him. There was decision and strength and command in the set of his bearded jaw, breeding and intelligence in his clear eyes and well-proportioned brow.

Jorn Javas found him at the wheel. He had tied himself to it with thongs from his warrior's harness, bound himself into position with great cunning. His hands, black and swollen now from lack of circulation, were clamped onto the spokes of the wheel, and he was slumped across it, his head fallen upon his chest.

A start of pure horror went through the young officer as he gazed on this man . . . *for he knew him!*

It was Norgovan Thul, lord high Admiral of Tsargol!

But Norgovan Thul had sailed for Vozashpa days ago in the company of Prince Karm Karvus, lord of the City, aboard the *Crown of Tsargol,* flagship of the fleet, the Prince's own ship . . . a great trireme very much like this one. But this charnel ship, crewed with the dead and with the living dead, befouled with blood and wreckage, could not be the proud gilded trireme that had put to sea days before, bearing the Prince of Tsargol on a visit-of-state to the throne of Vozashpa . . . *or could it?*

His heart in his mouth, the pale young officer turned to look about the deck with a dawning comprehension in his eyes. That brightwork on the afterdeck, that frieze of gilt and carven dolphins running along the rail—his gaze flashed to the door of the great cabin and saw embossed thereupon the crossed sword-and-anchor that was the royal emblem of Tsargol, her standard and ensign.

It was then that the full impact of the awful truth crashed upon the mind of Jorn Javas.

On unsteady legs he crossed the cadaver-strewn deck to the door of the great cabin. With nerveless and trembling fingers he fumbled at the lock. The great carven door swung open slowly and Jorn Javas peered within, dreading what he might see . . . for if sudden insanity and inexplicable death had struck down the crew and officers of the royal flagship, how could the Prince have survived untouched by either the red hand of murder or the white touch of madness?

But the cabin was empty.

The Otar searched it from wall to wall, but he found not the body of Karm Karvus.

Slowly he made his way back to the deck and to the place where the body of Norgovan Thul was tied to the wheel.

The Admiral was not dead, as Jorn Javas had first surmised. For the older man lifted his head and turned his face, smeared with a ghastly dew of mingled sweat and blood, at the young officer. He peered at Jorn Javas with wide haunted eyes through a matted tangle of wet locks.

"My Lord . . . you live? What . . . happened here?" he asked.

The reply came slowly in a dull croaking voice.

". . . The Gray Death . . . the Gray Death . . ." the Admiral groaned.

Jorn Javas cut the other down with his blade, slicing through the thongs which bound him to his post, thongs which had sunk deeply into his flesh and which had left cruel marks therein. He eased the older man to a place on the deck, pillowed the man's head on his knees and gave him to drink of water from the cannister at his hip.

"But the Prince, our lord Karm Karvus, what of him? *Speak*, man!"

Norgovan Thul had fought off madness with all the strength in him. With the last dregs of his iron endurance, fighting to hold to his sanity, the brave old Admiral had forced the ship about and guided her into port—an ordeal of such superhuman effort that the imagination shrinks from picturing it. For days, while the demons of madness nibbled at the edges of his mind, the loyal old Tsargolian had driven what few men remained alive to their oars by the sheer force of his will. But the effort had taken a ghastly toll. His strength was drained. No longer could he hold firm the citadel of his reason against the gibbering shadows that plucked and tore at the very center of his being. He smiled horribly, slack-jawed as an idiot. His haunted eyes rolled back in his head. Jorn Javas shook him fiercely, demanding again to know what had happened to Karm Karvus. But all the Admiral could say was one word, over and over and over again:

"Gone . . . gone . . . *gone . . . !*"

And when the other officers of the Tsargolian Guard summoned their courage and followed the brave young Otar to the bloody deck, they found Jorn Javas sitting amidst the corpses, the head of the Admiral still pillowed on his knee. The Admiral tossed and turned his head, mouthing meaningless words which broke betimes into mindless howling, like the other madmen who still lived aboard this nightmare ship.

The grizzled old Daotar seized Jorn Javas by the shoulder. The young man raised his tear-wet face to his superior.

"Did he say anything?" the Daotar demanded. "Is our lord Prince aboard the vessel?"

The youth shook his head in despair.

"Gone . . . *gone*," he said hopelessly.

*

IN the absence of Prince Karm Karvus, the Lord Chancellor Drath Horvan, Baron of Amagar, as senior peer of the realm and senior officer of state, wielded the powers of a regent.

Within mere minutes of the discovery of the derelict and its crew of madmen and the dead, an emergency council of state was held in the Palace of Tsargol. Grim-eyed and white-faced peers and high commanders debated the meaning of the terrible events of the night, and the implications thereof. The *Crown of Tsargol* had been searched from stem to stern, but no clues had been discovered which might explain the strange and terrible tragedy. As for those found aboard—and they were but a fraction of the crew, for many were missing—they were either dead or incurably mad. From the dead there was nothing that could be learned, save that they had died either at their own hands or before the maddened attacks of their own shipmates. Nor was aught to be learned from the living, for they were not capable of rational converse.

The only fragment of information that was gleaned

from the babblings of the howling men was the single phrase which many of them repeated over and over—

The Gray Death . . . the Gray Death.

But what that mysterious and enigmatic phrase might mean, none could say. If, indeed, it meant anything at all, and was not merely the mindless mumbling of men driven over the edges of reason into the red chaos of insanity.

What was it that had driven a shipful of men insane? And what of Karm Karvus? Was the Prince dead or alive? And, if he yet lived, was he, too, among the howling chorus of the mad?

He was not found aboard the *Crown,* and he was among the many mariners missing from the full complement of the crew. The councillors debated what could have happened to these men. The most logical answer was that, being raving maniacs, they had flung themselves into the sea in their madness and fury.

"The *Crown* could not have reached Vozashpa in time to return," Drath Horvan mused grimly. "At best, with favorable winds, the voyage consumes seven days. And there is nothing between Tsargol and Vozashpa, save empty beaches and forested wilderness, no town, no settlement of men. The thing, whatever it was, that drove the men into madness must have struck while they were upon the high seas. And since our Prince was not found on board, alas, we are forced to the conclusion that he fell or threw himself into the immeasurable waves of Yashengzeb Chun . . ."

Silent faces and lowered eyes around the council table gave back no argument in counter to this supposition. Drath Porvis bit his lip savagely, his brow furrowed.

"What is yet to be discovered is whether this tragedy is some grim freak of nature, to be listed among the many mysteries of the unknown sea, or perchance the planned and deliberate attack of some cunning enemy as yet undeclared. For—" his voice sank to a whisper "—*magic* could have worked this terror."

The council ended without deciding anything, like most councils. But Tsargol was on the alert, and keen-eyed guards watched from tower-top and wall, at gate and avnue and to seawards, alert for the slightest sign of any enemy. If this was but the prelude to an assault, it would find the red stone city by the sea armed and ready.

And from the landing stages atop the mighty Palace of Tsargol, where a contingent of the Air Guard of Patanga was stationed, a lone ship rose with the first light of dawn, bearing within its small cabin a Patangan pilot and a royal Tsargolian herald.

The slim little flying boat rose into the dawn above the unsleeping city, circled once, and sped off to north and east, hurtling through the clear skies of morning like a silver arrow to bear the word of the loss of Karm Karvus to the throne of Thongor the Mighty, the Lord of the West of the World.

CHAPTER 2:

BLACK HAWK'S RING

Had some grim, black and unknown doom
Struck bold Karm Karvus—and had he
Gone to an unmarked, nameless tomb
Beneath the dragon-haunted sea?

—Thongor's Saga, Stave XIX

NEAR midnight a day after the Gray Death first struck and the half-wrecked trireme limped into Tsargol harbor, a second ship glided into port many leagues to the north and east of that red stone city.

Here, at the head of the Gulf of Patanga, at the mouth of the Twin Rivers, rose the great metropolis of Patanga—the seat of Thongor the Mighty and the most powerful of the Nine Cities of the West.

But this second vessel was no princely trireme, gilded and caparisoned for a king's pleasure. It was long and low and rakish, with a lean black hull. Scarlet sails caught the gusting wind and a sharp prow cleaved the brine with ominous silent speed. And there were live, sane men aboard, not howling madmen. They crowded the rails for a glimpse of High Patanga in the glory of the moon.

A captain of the Air Guards glimpsed the lean black galley as she glided into port. No signal lamps flared in all her slim black length, and she had the look of a pirate about her. The airboat circled about, lamps flashing code signals to watchmen atop the mighty Air Citadel which rose east of the Great Plaza at Patanga's heart. Horns rang out—messengers clattered on kroter-back down the broad Thorian Way to the Sea Gate to give the alarm.

Thus it was, when the slim dark galley drew in to dock, half a company of the Patangan Archers were waiting, faces grim under the light of streaming torches. The Otar of the company strode forward to hail the unknown intruder from the midnight sea.

"Ahoy the black galley! Your name, port and master?"

Faces lined the gunwales—a ragtail crew, scrapings of the gutters of half the cities of the West. There was a fat, moon-faced Kovian, a gaudy kerchief wound about his brows; brown, black-haired Turanians and Cadornyana with amber skins and almond eyes—even one of the mighty Blue Nomads from the limitless plains of the ultimate West. They looked to be a motley crew of ruffians, glittering with gems and baubles, some marked with cutlass scars and some branded with outlawry. And sash and girdle bristled with weapons.

Then a big hand shoved them aside and cleared space for a towering redbeard with a bright crimson kerchief about his brows, breeches of bottle-green, enormous black boots and a massive, gem-encrusted girdle. His bare bronze chest bristled with fleece of curly gold and frosty gray eyes blazed under tufted brows. He was a bull of a man with deep chest, broad shoulders, and arms that bulged with knotted thews like the branches of a gnarled oak.

"This be the *Scimitar* out of Tarakus port," he growled, "and I be Barim Redbeard, her master."

The young officer tightened his jaw. "The pirates of Tarakus will find no welcome in the City of the Flame. Why do you slink by night into our harbor like some skulking thief?"

Barim Redbeard grinned, white teeth flashing amidst the fiery bush of his whiskers. "The fewer that know my mission the better, lad! But I be certain o' my welcome in the Fire City: here—catch!"

He withdrew a small object from his girdle and tossed

it. It flashed in the torchlight, a golden thing. The young Otar snatched it out of the air with a deft hand and turned it over, peering curiously.

It was a heavy ring of massy gold. Cut deep in the bevel were two glyphs in the pictographic writing of the Southlands; the Ka Thon and the Gor Yaa, these two glyphs were called, and they looked like this:

The Otar blinked with astonishment. He could not believe the testimony of his eyes, and on the rail above, the burly Redbeard chuckled at his reaction.

"Thongor!" the officer gasped.

"Aye," the pirate grinned. "The Lord Thongor's name cut in the solid gold of Patanga. 'Twas the Great King himself give me that bauble, that ever I needed word with him, the showing of it at his gate would bring me swift into his presence."

The Otar was nonplussed. There were but ten such rings in all the world, great seal rings that bore the name of the Lord of the Six Cities, and it was kings and princes bore them, high lords who bowed to the Black Hawk Banner. Such rings were keys and they gave instant access to the person of Thongor at any hour.

The young officer stiffened and saluted the grinning corsair as if he were a Prince of the Empire.

"You bear the Seal of Thongor, Captain, and I am yours to command. Come with me and I will bring you before the Lord of the West . . ."

*

BARIM had seen palaces before, and he did not pause to stare at the glistening marbles, the banners of rippling gold, or the glory of splendid spires athwart the star-gemmed sky.

But he checked his stride and his eyes widened at the sight of the young boy who stood at the palace gate, grinning, eager, hands outstretched in greeting.

"Lad, is it yourself? So big and tall, why, I had hardly like to have recognized my little shipmate in the likes of this grown lad!" he marveled.

Prince Thar laughed with delight.

"Of course I've grown, Captain Barim—it's been three years, you know, since we sailed together that time Charn Thovis bore me away from the usurper, Dalendus Vool, and you helped us get away.* It is wonderful to see you again! But what brings you to my father's capital, in such secrecy and by night?"

The Redbeard sobered. "Dark business lad, aye, black and dire. But surely you remember your old shipmates, here . . ."

His companions came pushing up behind him, crowding the son of Thongor on every side, grinning affectionately.

"Ye'll still be remembering fat old Blay, I trust," wheezed a jovial, moonfaced Kovian, dirks bristling from a vast leathern girdle that encircled his mighty paunch.

"And Durgan, too, I hope!" whined a lean, leathery old rogue with a black patch over one eye.

"Of course—and Thangmar, too!" the boy crowed, catching sight of a grinning giant from the Red Forests of Kodanga, his gold mane in a thick braid slung over powerful shoulders. "How wonderful to see all of you again. You haven't changed a bit!"

"But you have, aye, let me look at you," Barim boomed, holding the youth at arm's length. Thar had grown from the mischievous nine-year-old boy he remembered to a tall strong lad of twelve. His hard bronzed body was tough and sinewy and well-muscled for his years, and his square-jawed face, strange gold eyes and unshorn black mane were the very image of his mighty sire.

* You will find the story of this adventure told in a book called *Thongor at the End of Time*, published in 1968.

The captain tousled his hair and cuffed him fondly. "Ah, you were just a mite of a lad, then—now ye be half-way to being a man! But, come, have ye grown a prophet's skill these three years? How is't we find you waiting for us here?"

"A messenger rode on ahead to say you were following," Prince Thar said. And then he sobered, too. "But I forgot—they are waiting for you within—do you have some word of my father's friend, Karm Karvus?"

Barim looked puzzled and shook his head. "The Prince o' Tsargol? Why, flay me, lad, I know naught of his doings. 'Tis on another matter I'd have speech with the Lord Thongor."

"Very well. My father left word you were to be admitted the moment you arrived. Come, I will lead the way . . ."

*

THE Hall of the Hundred Kings was vast and shadowy. Huge pillars rose, supporting a domed roof far overhead. The floor of the mighty hall was paved with squares of polished marble, black and gold. Motionless guards in the black leather and gold helms of Thongor's own hand-picked regiment, the famous Black Dragons, stood evenly spaced the length of the hall. Massive candelabra that stood as tall as men shed fierce light, flashing on burnished gold shields charged held by the guards and glittered from polished helm and lance-head. In a circle about the edge of the great dome, stone faces brooded down on the tense scene below. Some of the marble visages were bearded and kingly, some bore the features of martial conquerors.

The stony portraits of the Hundred Kings of Patanga stared down at their heir and successor, throned amid the splendor of his brilliant court—the Lord Thongor himself.

The Flame Throne of Patanga was sheathed in beaten gold the color of flame. Flame-like, too, was the ornamentation of that throne, whose high back rose to wavy, flamy points. Atop a nine-tiered dais of black marble stood the Flame Throne, and thereupon sate Thongor.

He was a magnificent lion of a man, with the broad

shoulders and mighty chest and splendid thews of some savage gladiator. His grim dark face was impassive, expressionless, but under his black scowling brows his strange gold eyes blazed lion-like.

Robed was he in black imperial velvet. The gold shield of Patanga was upon his breast, charged with the Black Hawk of Valkarth, his savage Northlander home.

Naked, across his thighs lay the great Valkarthan broadsword wherewith he had hewn a red path to the Throne of the West. *Sarkozan*—Kingmaker—the old pre-Sanskrit Purānas name that mighty blade.

Binding his unshorn warrior's mane of coarse black hair, the Flame Crown was upon his brow. The wavy points of it flashed with huge chandrals, a rare Lemurian gem whose gold-orange crystals matched the fiery hues of the golden coronal.

This night Thongor sat long at council with his peers. Slim, sardonic Prince Dru, bluff old Lord Mael, Baron Selverus and the Hierarch Eodrym—they all were there, as were those war-comrades, Zad Komis, Lord of the Black Dragons, and Thom Pervis of the Air Guard. And with them, a mighty Rmoahal giant, his indigo hide glistening, towered in war-harness beside a young Turanian with smooth black hair and alert, intelligent eyes, his supple hard body clad in the black harness of the Dragons. These were Shangoth of the Jegga Nomads and young Charn Thovis.

Indeed, all of the great ones of Patanga were here save for the lovely Sumia, the Empress. With her, motherhood took precedence over affairs of state, for a girl-child had been born to Thongor's mate scarce a year before, and the babe—a little Princess named after Sumia's mother, Zandarla—demanded full attention.

It was the young warrior noble, Charn Thovis, who first saw Barim Redbeard and his comardes as they came striding into the great hall with Prince Thar as their guide. The young officer grinned and rose to greet the corsairs, for it had been he, three years ago, who helped the Prince escape the clutches of the scheming Dalendus Vool. They had found refuge aboard the *Scimitar* and made firm friends.

On the Flame Throne, Thongor, his frowning brow

heavy, his grim jaw resting on one balled fist, pondered the mystery of Karm Karvus, one of his oldest comrades. Now his brow cleared, a rare smile lit his somber features, as Redbeard strode up to the throne.

"Redbeard—by Gorm and All Gods!" he thundered, rising from his kingly chair and descending to clap the grinning corsair on one burly shoulder. "I see the dragons of the deep have not yet breeched the *Scimitar*'s black hull—'tis good to see you, man!"

Introductions were made all around and scurrying pages fetched seats and chilled wine for Barim and his men.

"We sit late at council, pondering the fate of my good friend, the Prince of Tsargol," Thongor said when the pirates were settled comfortably. "When the docks sent word the *Scimitar* was come in secret to my shores, I bethought me you brought some word to shed light on the mystery of his vanishment."

Barim shook his fiery mane. "Alas, Lord, the first I heard of this was from the lad himself—*harrumph!*—the young Jasark your princely son, I mean. 'Tis on another business am I come, with strange and evil tidings . . . but I would know of this Tsargol matter, ere I disgorge mine own tale."

In terse, grim words Thongor sketched in what little was known of the weird doom that had befallen Karm Karvus at sea; and one phrase of his account wrung a grunt of astonishment from the Redbeard.

"The Gray Death, is it? *Hai,* Gods, I am come in great good time," he growled, and fat Blay and wry Durgan and huge Thangmar muttered amongst themselves. Thongor demanded his meaning.

"That already 'tis begun; and best I delay no more in unlading what knowledge I bring hither. Aye, sink me for a merchantman, would I had come days earlier, then might your friend Karvus have been spared!"

"Explain," Thongor said curtly.

"Aye, Lord. Then here's the lot . . ." And in rough words, all interspersed with sailor-oaths, he unfolded a strange and awesome tale before his noble audience.

*

FROM their impregnable stronghold at the end of a rocky promontory that thrust from the base of the Gulf into the Southern Sea, the bold corsairs of Tarakus had ravished the main for half a century.

The swift and deadly pirate fleet made Tarakus master of the seas, and in time the lawless realm of sea-going rogues grew more daring and audacious till at last the lean black ships struck at whole cities, pillaging the ports of the South without fear of reprisal. Like lightning they would strike, slim black hulls closing in like sharks for the kill—struck, and were gone to impregnable Tarakus the Pirate City ere slower naval vessels could pursue.

All this Thongor well knew, for years before, when he had been a roving adventurer, long ere Chance or Fate or Heaven raised him to the highest throne of the West, he had ravened with the sea wolves of Tarakus. A Captain of the Red Brotherhood, the bold Valkarthan had sailed his ship, the *Black Hawk,* from Tarakus to loot the high seas of gold and wine and treasure.

Eighteen years had past since those wild, lawlesss days. The pirate city had grown since his time. A savage and ambitious leader had arisen to goad the corsairs to new enormities—Kashtar, Red Wolf of Tarakus, men called him. Wealth, mere gold, did not suffice to sate his furious hunger . . . he would win thrones, kingdoms—an empire! Scowling grimly, Thongor listened as Barim concluded.

" 'Twas when this renegade wizard, Belshathla, sought haven in Tarakus that Kashtar found the means to sate his lust for power," Barim's growled. "The magicker came out o' the wastelands of Nianga where the buried cities be—the ones the Gods whelmed and trod down aeons ago for some great crime against the world. This Belshathla brought with him some black secret—some weird weapon from Earth's Dawn—stolen from a Niangan tomb, belike, or looted from the rubble of the accursed cities. Whatever the thing be, 'tis given the Red Wolf courage to strive for the greatest prize of all . . ." His voice sank to a whisper and they bent near to catch his next words.

"*. . . Patanga itself!*"

Cries of outrage, astonishment, denial rang out. Zad Komis swore a grim oath: "This is madness! True, the pirate rabble have a strong fleet—but to assault the mightiest city on Earth? 'Tis madness, I say! They have no chance of success."

Grizzled Thom Pervis, Daotarkon of the Air Guard, agreed. "We are impregnable to attack, Sire! What fleet, however strong, can stand against our flying navy—armed with the lightning guns our wise young sage Iothundus has perfected!"

Lord Mael, one of Thongor's most loyal peers, growled acknowledgment of this. " 'Twas proven, Sire, some twelve or eleven years ago at the Battle of Tsargol when we broke the force of Yelim Pelorvis; and won a throne for young Karm Karvus. The flying boats make us invincible. The conventional measures of strength—a huge fleet, a mighty host—are naught against our power in the skies."

Thongor was impassive, his strange gold eyes wary and thoughtful.

"I would know more of this weapon," he grunted, "ere I speak of being unconquerable."

CHAPTER 3:

THE GRAY MAGICIANS

"Now in these days of his greatness was
Thongor supreme among the lords of the
world, and in the fulness of his power
there was no king in all the land of
Lemuria who had the might to stand against
the Lord of the West of the World . . ."

—The Lemurian Chronicles, Book 5, Chapter III.

AEDIR the Sun-god rose high above Patanga and all the land was bright with morning. Shortly after dawn, the Lord Thongor and his peers were met a second time. With dawn the Hierarch had sent messengers to beg their attendance upon him in the priestly palace that rose on the southern side of the central plaza at the city's heart. All that night had Father Eodrym searched through crumbling scrolls and ancient books, seeking some clue as to the lost wisdom of Nianga, some hint as to what the weird weapon from Time's Dawn might be.

They met in his vast librarium, a great room of high ceilings, the walls covered with thousands of mighty tomes. Some were writ on sheets of tanned leather, bound between carved wood or ivory boards; others were scrolls of pterodactyl-hide, etched with metallic inks; yet more were yellow, wrinkled vellum, sealed with iron hasps. The wisdom of a thousand ages slumbered in this quiet room.

Weary from a sleepless night, the frail old Hierarch met them seated in a great chair of black and carven wood, drawn up before a bookstand whereon a mighty volume lay open. The leaves of this ponderous volume were thin sheets of perdurable metal worked in fiery acids, and thus proof against the assaults of time.

"Sire, and my Lords," the old man spake in a thin, exhausted voice, "I have begged your presence here to divulge certain discoveries I have made which bear both on the disappearance of the Prince of Tsargol and the ominous threat of this Niangan sorcerer."

He laid one frail hand on the great book that lay open on the lectern before him.

"This is that mighty book of records known as *The Lemurian Chronicles,*" he said. "Somewhat of this volume you may have heard 'ere now, for it is the mightiest book of all the ages. I possess the only copy that still exists in the West, and therein have I found a strange and shadowy tale of ancient horrors . . ."

*

AS they sat listening, the old Hierarch told a curious tale in his faint, exhausted voice.

He told of an ancient collegium of sages who dwelt in a secret monastery hidden in a far land . . . a mystical fraternity known as the Pnothic Brotherhood. From the age of the First Kingdoms of Man, the Seven Cities of the East, these wise seers had explored the limitless expanse of Eternity by means of a difficult mind discipline called the Akashic Science. Past, present and future they delved into, and the fruit of their mystical quest was a vast epitome of the history of the Universe which was set down in this age-old book.

"The Pnothic Brethren see all of time as the single history of one eternal conflict which they have named The Wars of Chaos and Creation," the Hierarch murmured. "In the dark, howling Chaos that lies beyond the frontiers of Creation, malign forces of destruction and doom strive ever to extinguish the Universe . . . ever the Lords of Creation battle to preserve Creation against Chaos . . . and this eternal war hath been fought ere now on many worlds, in aeons lost to memory.

"The planets of heaven, say the sages, are worlds much like unto our own, and life exists on some of these. Was a world once named Zarkandu where Chaos begot a mighty Son, and long the kings and heroes of that lost world of time fought to preserve the empire they had builded. At length they won and Chaos' Son they destroyed, but the Dark Powers triumphed in the end and all that world was wrecked, and now but frozen rubble mark its place in the trackless void. The battle of the eternal War was lost . . . and on another world, which we call Iridar, Chaos subverted a dark immortal Flame Being to evil, and again heroes strove against the tides of Chaos and Old Night, and won, but in the passing of many ages fair, garden-girdled Iridar was drained of life and now floats on the void a dead world of crimson deserts, where a thin wind sifts dry red sand across the broken thrones of forgotten cities . . .

"On our world, too, this War is being fought. You know the tale, my Lords, and the *Lemurian Chronicles* preserve the annals of Hyperborea in her prime, that ruled the Age of Reptiles ere the coming of Man. Chaos seduced the Dragon Kings of that dim dawn age to vile sorcery, and the Lords of Life wrought Man, and Man and Dragon fought in The Thousand Year War and at length the Dragon fell and the Age of Men began. The Seven Cities rose . . . but Chaos, abandoning the Brood of the Serpent, tempted Zaar and all that city turned to evil wizardry. The Seven Cities fell and the raw young cities of the West rose . . . and again Chaos tempted men with subtle sciences, this time in Nianga, which lieth between East and West . . ."

Old Father Eodrym told of the Aeon of the Gray Magicians, wherein the three cities of Nianga strove to master the dark sciences and by that mastery to dominate the Earth. This was thirty centuries before the age of Thongor, and little his age knew of those dark days. The three cities of Kuth and Shandathar and grim Zanjan learned many of the secrets of Creation, aye, even dared to tamper with that force which sustains the Earth amidst the firmament, and with the secrets locked in the fiery heart of the Sun itself. And, as the *Scarlet Edda* whispers, they mastered a gray magic which gave them control over the human mind, to hold it prisoned in terrible slavery or to shatter it to madness, if such be their whim.

But the Nineteen Gods struck them down in their blasphemy and trod their cities into dust, and all their land was laid waste and their people fled in terror . . . but who can say what dread secrets lay buried in the ruins of those lost cities . . . secrets which mayhap the cunning Belshathla had brought to light again, to lay all this new age in peril with the terrible menace of an evil lore?

*

THE trembling voice of the old Hierarch stilled and with a reverent hand he closed the mighty book and locked the nineteen seals wherewith it was secured against the prying eyes of the unworthy.

A thoughtful silence followed upon the reading of that solemn passage of Elder Lore.

The strange gold eyes of Thongor blazed with wrathful fires like the savage eyes of the kingly vandar of the wild, the great black lion of ancient Lemuria.

"And again, Chaos," he growled. "Will we never be done with the taint of the dark powers! It has been six long years since we whelmed the Black City of Zaar before the sithurl-guns and let the waters of the sea cover it from the sight of men, and still it haunts us!"

"My son," the old Hierarch said somberly, "the Wars of Chaos and Creation have been fought from the beginning of Time unto this very hour, and the end is not in sight. Chaos and Creation battled on the lost planet of Zarkandu one hundred million years ago, nor did they end even when the Divine Avatar, Sargon the Lion, whelmed the Black God's Son. Neither did they end on age-lost Iridar ten million years ago, when Chandar broke the Dark Flame, or when his mighty son, Arn, secured the Sword of Psamathis and the Three Talismans were preserved from the grip of Chaos. Nor did the War of unending aeons close when you broke down the walls of Black Zaar. Of this War we shall not see the ending in our time, nay, nor for uncounted ages to come . . ."

*

AEDIR the Sun-god had long since ascended to the zenith of the noon and now inclined his fiery orb to the west. The long shadows lay thick on the broad avenues of Patanga. And within the Palace of the Hundred Kings, Thongor sprawled like a great cat before a blazing hearth, his infant daughter in his arms.

His mate, Sumia, regarded him with great dark eyes. Solemn was the gaze thereof, and they brimmed with unshed tears, like wet black jewels. But the Sarkaja did not give way to those tears but held them in.

"Thus I have no choice," Thongor growled. "It was the benison of Tiandra, Goddess of Fortune, that permitted the stout old Redbeard to bear advance warning of the plans of Tarakus to me in time. Barim says the invasion will be soon—terribly soon—but that we have yet some several days of freedom wherein to work against the plot of Kashtar Red Wolf. That margin of time may prove precious indeed, for much may be accomplished in even so few days, by daring and desperate men."

"But why must you venture into the streets of Tarakus alone?" Sumia asked, her calm voice betraying no sign of the turmoil within her heart. "Surely it is reckless to the point of madness to thrust yourself into the very hands of your greatest enemies! Why not pass the word to Thom Pervis, and strike first against Tarakus with all the might of our sky navy—a sudden, unexpected stroke that would bring the strength of the Pirate City down before they even guessed the Empire was forewarned?"

Her mate regarded her with thoughtful eyes.

"There is wisdom in your words, my girl, but I dare not try it. Suppose the pirates of Tarakus turn the Gray Death against the airboats and destroy them . . . the last hope of

Patanga fails, then, even before the corsair fleet sets forth upon the seas. No! We of Valkarth have an old adage—'Trust not all your arrows in one quiver, lest it be lost and your bow go empty in the hour of need.' I shall ship aboard the *Scimitar* with Redbeard and no man shall know me for the King, for who would dream the Lord of the Six Cities would venture alone into the stronghold of the corsairs, rather than sit safely throned amidst all his warriors? Now, Kashtar knoweth not that Barim Redbeard is my friend, and the *Scimitar* can come into the very harbor of Tarakus without giving alarm. Thus shall I gain entry to the Pirate City and, mayhap, by aid of Redbeard and his trusty crew, work mighty mischief on the Red Wolf and his Gray Magician, to the saving of Patanga itself, perchance, if the luck of the Gods be with me at my need."

The Princess made no further protest to his going-forth. There was a certain wisdom in his words, though perhaps the weight of sober reason and responsibility resided in her own arguments against his going. But she knew her savage mate well, and she knew the restlessness that seethed within him, and how he hungered for action and adventure. More than once had he referred to himself during these long years of peace and kingship, as a bright, keen-edged sword that was left rusting in neglect. Her woman's heart knew well the nature of her man. The long, adventurous, roving years he had spent as wandering swordsman, thief, pirate and bandit chief, ere destiny had lifted him to the height of the mightiest throne of all the West, had instilled deep within him the lust of battle and action. And so she did not argue further against his going.

"When will you sail, then?" she asked.

"With dawn," he grunted.

She smiled, and stretched languidly, and her slim white hands went up to the massed midnight sheen of her tresses. Slowly, her great dark eyes on his, she began to undo her hair.

"There are yet many hours until dawn," she whispered, and smiled to see the fires that leapt up in his eyes as he set the babe aside and rose lithely to crush her in his mighty arms.

CHAPTER 4:

DRAGONS OF THE DEEP

From hidden reef and fickle wind
And changeful tides, preserve us;
And from the dragons of the deep,
O Father Gorm, preserve us.

—Lemurian Seamens' Prayer

AS the first faint glory of dawn flamed golden in the east, a slim black galley crept from the harbor of Patanga and set forth on the waters of the Gulf.

Scarlet sails spread wide to catch the morning wind, the black ship clove the dark waters almost without a sound to mark its passage, save for the creak of the timbers, the snap of booming sails, and the moaning cry of the wind in the rigging.

Morning mist roiled, thick and white, upon the face of the waters. Stars still burned in the darkness of the sky, but steadily, moment by moment, glory grew brighter in the east and shafts of burning light thrust across the gloom of heaven, driving the stars to rest. And it was day.

A brisk wind snapped the cordage. The tang of salt spray was in the gust and stung the lips of Thongor as the great Barbarian strode the decks of the *Scimitar*. It had been years since the mighty Valkarthan had bestrode a quarterdeck, and he was glad that his years of court and palace life had not taken away his seamanship. He grinned hugely, black mane tossing in the salt wind, and his deep chest expanded as he drank in great breaths of the clean, briny air. *Hai—Gorm!* 'Twas a good thing to be alive, in the full strength of his prime, and setting forth to new adventure on the high seas, with a good ship under him and stout and proven comrades at his side.

Dour, lean old Durgan was at the wheel and Thongor greeted him. As for Barim Redbeard, the corsair captain of the *Scimitar* was at the aft rail, drinking in the salt wind and snorting lustily. The redbearded giant was stripped to the waist, save for a boat cloak slung across his broad shoulders and the baldric across his chest. Thongor, too, had tossed aside his robes of imperial velvet and gladly donned again the plain leathern harness of a wandering Lemurian warrior.

Black boots clad him to the knee. A loincloth of scarlet hung for his ornate girdle. A broad leathern collar encircled his mighty throat and his bronzed and mighty chest was bare save for the straps of a warrior's trappings. A great black cloak, pinned to the shoulders of the broad collar, with cairngorm broaches, swelled with the wind behind him like vast black wings. Sarkozan, his great Valkarthan broadsword, swung in its scabbard at his side, and pocket-pouch and dirk completed the total of his accouterments.

Barim spied him as the Barbarian strode grinning across the deck to where the captain stood at the rail. Snorting and beaming affably, the Redbeard hailed him.

"A fine day, eh lad? *Kerhem!* I mean, Sire—ah, my Lord—"

Thongor grinned, white teeth flashing in his dark face.

"No titles, Redbeard! Here you are captain and I, but a member of the crew. And, mayhap, since we plan to enter Tarakus without revealing who I am, 'twould be better to forget the name under which I am Lord of the Six Cities."

"Flay me, but 'tis a worthy notion, man," Barim rumbled. "What name, then, shall we use for ye?"

Humor flashed in Thongor's strange gold eyes.

"Now, let me think! When I fought as one of the pirates of Tarakus many years ago, they called me *Khongrim*—the Black Hawk. Let me be named Black Hawk, then, whilst aboard the *Scimitar*—eh?"

"Black Hawk, it is," the Redbeard nodded.

The deck planks creaked behind them and they turned to see the young *kojan,* Charn Thovis, climb the stairs that led to the quarterdeck. The dragon helm and jeweled harness of the Black Dragons, wherein the young warrior was a high officer in command of a thousand troops, had been set aside for the duration of this voyage. Charn Thovis wore simple black leather studded with gray iron, even as did Thongor. He hailed his Lord and Captain Redbeard deferentially.

Of all his nobles, lords and warriors, Thongor had chosen young Charn Thovis alone to accompany him on this perilous voyage. Perhaps he had made his choice because, three years before, when this youth had rescued Prince Thar from the clutches of Dalendus Vool and carried the boy out of the city, Charn Thovis had sailed on the *Scimitar*. It was the young warrior who had won over the captain and crew of the black corsair galley to the protection of the Jasark. His words, and the winning ways of the brave young Prince, had been equally responsible for turning the hearts of the *Scimitar* pirates.

And there had been one other factor as well. For Barim Redbeard was no native of the Dakshina, the Southlands, but one of Thongor's own countrymen. The redbearded warrior had been born and bred in the wintry wastelands of the barren North—in Belnarth on the shores of Zharanga Tethrabaal the Great North Ocean. Belnarth lay not far from Thongor's own savage homeland of Valkarth beyond Eobar. And, although Thongor was the last of his people, the Black Hawk clan, Redbeard's own tribe, the White Wolf people of Belnarth, were their ancient friends, clan-brothers bound by old ties of blood-kinship. Northlandermen were rarely found below the Mountains of Mommur, and they tended to stand together when the arrow was broken and red war roared.

Charn Thovis was also grinning, happy to be aboard ship again with his old comrades—and proud that Thongor the Mighty had chosen him out of ten thousand warriors to fight at his side. As they exchanged good-mornings, fat, friendly Blay thrust his red, perspiring moonface up the steps of the quarterdeck and hailed them.

"Ha, Cap'n—Lords! Cook says to come below, the mornin' meal be ready, and 'twill fast grow cold an you come not to table in all haste," he wheezed.

They adjourned to the great cabin where Barim Redbeard slept. It was huge and untidy, a long, low-roofed chamber, with great wooden beams from which horn lanterns dangled, and diamond-paned windows that opened out on the rudder and the white wake. Barim had offered the great cabin to his regal guest, but Thongor—or *Khon-*

grim as he had named himself for the duration of this adventure—refused to drive Barim from his own quarters, preferring to share a cabin with Thangmar, the blond Kodanga. As for Charn Thovis, he was pleased to share quarters with the Rmoahal, Roegir, for the two of them had become fast friends during their first voyage together.

A large folding table had been set up in the great cabin, and Thongor, Charn Thovis, Redbeard and his first mate, a peevish, black-avised little officer named Angar Zend, sat them down to a huge breakfast. Broiled fish in lemon sauce, fresh fruit and hot buttered bread, cold carved fowl and spiced boars-flesh, great slabs of tangy cheese, and ripe brown ale in cups of gold thieved from the belly of a rich merchant galley out of Shembis—all this and more was set upon the table. The fresh salt air had given them all a hearty appetite, and they fell to like true trenchermen.

*

ALL that day and night, and the next day as well, the lean black galley with the dragon-beaked prow of burnished brass and the great scarlet sails rode the winds ever south.

The great Gulf of Patanga cleft the Lemurian continent almost to its heart. There were many leagues of blue water to sail before the tall towers of Tarakus would rise on the horizon.

Gulls squawked and circled about their masts. White water foamed in their wake. The lean sharp prow of the galley, as knife-like as its very namesake, clove through the shining water like a slashing blade.

The walls of Patanga fell away astern and were lost in the distance. Hour after hour they cut through the briny waves. Another city of the Gulf, Thurdis, where Barand Thon ruled as Prince, hove into view along the western shores of the Gulf and fell away behind them. At the rail, Thongor and Charn Thovis watched as Shembis and Zangabal and finally Pelorm hove into view.

The great Gulf widened now as they neared its mouth, where the waters of the Gulf mingled with the wild waves of Yashengzeb Chun the Southern Sea. Only a few more leagues, now, ere they would come into view of Tarakus the Pirate City. Another night's sailing, and a few hours of daylight, and the *Scimitar* would drop anchor in the great harbor below the capitol of the corsair kingdom.

Then it was that Fate took a hand.

*

IT was a scrawny Turanian sailor, his bare brown back wealed with scars from the slave-galleys of Shembis, who saw the monster first. High atop the foremast was he stationed, for aloft in the upper rigging his keen eyes could see far through the gathering dusk. His bellow of alarm rang down from the masthead, and in a trice bare and booted feet thudded on the deck as all hands were summoned to battle stations.

Water broke a few hundred yards to port as a great scaled head lit with cold eyes of lambent flame rose above the surface of the Gulf.

Fat Blay sucked in his breath. Sour old Durgan squinted with his one good eye and muttered a prayer to the Sea God, Shastadion. Thangmar grimly tested the edge of his great sword and tall Roegir strung his terrible war bow. All about them, the battle-hardened pirate crew of the *Scimitar* prepared to fight for their lives against the Terror of the Deep.

For, in truth, it was one of the dread sea dragons of Lemuria. A mighty *larth,* cold eyes gleaming, floated on the waves to port, scaly dragon jaws open, revealing the glitter of its terrible fangs.

Seldom did the sea dragons of Yashengzeb Chun come this far up the Gulf, for the deeps of the high seas were their domain. But at certain seasons of the year the fish whereon they fed deserted the depths of the southern ocean and came up the Gulf to breed in the mouths of the rivers. Then the ravages of hunger drove the mighty reptilian monsters from their accustomed deeps . . . and then the sailors of old Lemuria had cause to pray to their green-bearded God of the Seas. For a full-grown *larth* is twice ship-size, and its lashing tail and titanic claws and terrible fanged jaws can tear a wooden galley asunder, or drag it beneath the waves.

Thongor stood on the quarterdeck, the great Valkarthan broadsword in his hand. Once, twelve years before, a tremendous storm had blown his airboat off course, into the waters of the lower Gulf—and he had been attacked by one of the mighty sea dragons of the deep. In that perilous hour, the Nineteen Gods had watched over his fortunes, and he and his comrades had escaped alive from the jaws of the Terror of the Deep. But if the dragon attacked the *Scimitar,* could he hope to escape a second time from the fangs of the savage and ferocious *larth?*

"Gorchak—Turan—Minga—man the catapults! Roegir, you great rogue, up into the rigging with you and your archers—fire arrows! All hands prepare to defend ship!"

Barim Redbeard, swearing lustily and dragging on battle-dress, roared orders to his pirates. Great traps were opened in the decks amidships. Pulleys creaked and groaned as sea catapults were hauled up into position. Heavy slugs of jagged stone or cast iron, which, in time of peace, served the *Scimitar* for ballast, were lifted into the arms of the powerful catapults. Capstans and windlasses groaned as the lines were drawn tight, and keen-eyed seamen measured height and windage and distance.

In these remote ages, long before the discovery of gunpowder or the invention of cannon, the Lemurian seamen had no other defense against the dragons of the sea save for these powerful catapults. A well-placed stone could, with luck, brain or maim or cripple even a full-grown *larth.* And many times, even though its scaly hide went unscathed by the deadly missiles, defensive action of this sort could frighten a dragon back into the waves.

But all knew that if the catapults failed, they were lost. For if once the dragon came at the galley itself, sword or spear or war arrow would have little effect upon that terrible reptilian engine of destruction. The mighty claws of the dragon could tear the decks apart, topple masts, stave in the hull.

For a time the *larth* paused, arched neck and jagged spine and blunt, serpent's head riding above the waves. It seemed to examine the ship, raking it with cold reptilian eyes that flamed like pits of yellow flame.

Then it gave voice to a harsh cry, and headed for the *Scimitar.* Almost in the same instant a sword came flashing down, cutting the taut line, and one of the catapults crashed skywards. The heavy missile went whirling through the twilight—and missed. A fountain of white foam gushed up to one side of the moving monster.

Twangg! Twunngg! The tight-bent arms of two more catapults flickered high, hurling their jagged and deadly burdens at the oncoming dragon. One grazed the gliding muscles of its shoulder, rousing a hiss of pain and rage. The other missed widely—

And the *larth* was upon them!

One great scaled paw closed on the rail. Timbers squealed and crunched as claws as huge as scimitars sunk deep in the hard wood. Like something out of a nightmare, the arched neck writhed into the twilight sky and the terrible head hung above the decks, eyes blazing like feral lamps through the dusk.

The dragon struck—once—twice! The head soared up again, a wriggling body clamped in the mighty jaws. The dragon crunched down, blood spurted in a grisly rain on the deck planks, the long snaky throat gulped down pulped flesh, and the head flashed out again, following a golden-skinned Cadornyan as he fled shrieking.

In a trice the jaws closed over another struggling body, and again blood squirted from the fanged jaws of the sea monster.

Arrows flickered from the rigging, but they could do little against the scaly hide of the dragon. Roegir plied his great bow tirelessly, and sent shaft after shaft whistling at the swinging head. But the barbed and deadly hail flickered, glancing from the tough mail of the monster.

Then the great head swung suddenly toward the place where Thongor stood, ready for action, broadsword glittering in one powerful fist.

It all happened so swiftly that it was done in no time. In the uncertain light, in the swift blur of movement, in the confusion of running, yelling, battling men, none could say exactly what had happened. Nor did Thongor have time to think, to plan, to reason. In a flashing instant, blind instinct drove him into whirlwind action.

The mighty Valkarthan leaped aside as the great head swung his way. To the rail in one great bound, then he sprang up and seized the rigging and hauled himself aloft. And—as the broad wedge-shaped head of the sea dragon swung by beneath him—he dropped down atop the dragon's head!

Before anyone could quite grasp the rapid sequence of events, the giant Barbarian sat astride the dragon's neck, powerful legs clamped together at its throat, just under the hinge of the lower jaw.

Bright steel flashed ruddy in the sunset flame as the great Valkarthan broadsword swung up—and came slashing down! Fetid reptilian gore oozed down the scaly jaws and the *larth* was convulsed with the stabbing pain of Thongor's mighty blow.

With the instincts of a born huntsman, Thongor struck again and again at one of the most vulnerable portions of the dragon's anatomy—the base of its skull, where the neck was narrow, the tough hide thin, and the spine exposed. If he could sever the dragon's spinal cord, the crippled monster could not wreck the pirate galley.

Again and again the great broadsword rose and fell, slashing ever deeper into the base of the spine.

Giving voice to a deafening bellow of pain and outrage, the mighty reptile released the *Scimitar*'s rail and swung away, sprawling in a smothering welter of flying foam.

Almost before Charn Thovis or Barim Redbeard could realize what had taken place, the writhing dragon was a hundred yards astern, slithering amidst shattering spray. The tiny figure of Thongor still clinging fast to its neck—the Valkarthan broadsword still chopping at the spine—the monster voiced one last shrill screech of fury—and sank from view, floundering beneath the roiling, white-foamed waters of the Gulf.

The dragon's tail rose once to smash the waves, then slithered through the wash of bubbling foam and was gone.

Gone, too, from the sight and the knowledge of men, was Thongor.

Silence fell like a pall over the blood-smeared and splinter-strewn decks of the pirate galley. The corsairs stared at one another in horror. Cold eyes softened; swarthy faces paled; hoarse voices muttered the names of their Gods.

Long they searched the seas about—long after daylight waned in a welter of crimson and darkness crept over the face of the deep. The longboats of the *Scimitar* combed the black waters, keen eyes searching each wave for some token of the bold Valkarthan. By lantern-glow and torch-light, they searched on, far into the night.

But when the great golden moon rose above the far edges of the earth to flood the Gulf with pale glory, Barim Redbeard called off the hunt. His face grim and impassive, his frosty eyes cold with dread, the great Red-beard knew in his heart of hearts 'twould do no good to search on into the darkness of the night.

The waves had swallowed the Warrior of the West, and only the Gods knew whither his indomitable spirit had flown . . . whether to the cold Shadowlands of the spirit world or the drowned black caverns of the unknown deep.

BOOK TWO

THE STORM BREAKS

"There be limitations set upon the inquiries of men, beyond which the Gods in their wisdom have forbidden man to seek knowledge. Nor have the High Gods set arbitrary borders to man's lawful curiosity . . . for vast forces beyond human comprehension move between the edges of Chaos and the shores of Creation, forces whereof the Gods themselves know but little and which neither God nor Demon dares to tamper with . . ."

—*The Scarlet Edda*

CHAPTER 5:

RED WOLF OF TARAKUS

And whether the Prince be alive or dead,
Could none in Tsargol say—
For none knew whether his soul was fled,
Nor where his body lay.

—The Tsargol Records

FOR days and nights beyond counting, Karm Karvus had lain in the foul dungeons beneath the towering bulk of the Pirate City, and he hungered for freedom. Freedom and—revenge!

When the squadron of corsair ships had struck suddenly from the darkness of the deep, his great trireme had had but little time to fight back. Like black wolves of the sea, the long slim hulls had closed in for the kill. The warriors aboard the great princely trireme drew naked steel and prepared to defend their Lord to the very gates of death itself . . . alas, the sea wolves of Tarakus had denied them even that privilege.

His lean jaw set grimly, his clear gray eyes bleak, the Prince of Tsargol remembered the terrible scene vividly. On the foredeck of the lead vessel a strange and outlandish contraption stood bolted to the planking. A fantastic thing it was, all globes of crystal and rods of twinkling brass. But from it struck a weird and terrible beam of gray light . . . colorless light that twisted the sight awry and held under some hypnotic fascination the minds of all they who had looked upon it.

With a terrific surge of iron will, the gallant Prince had torn his eyes from the shimmering hypnotic lamp. But his men, lords and nobles, courtiers and servants, officers and seamen, stood alike—staring at the source of gray throbbing luminance like men struck suddenly to stone by the unlidding of a Gorgon's eye.

The red wolves of Tarakus had swarmed aboard unopposed. Karm Karvus had fought mightily, but sheer weight of numbers had overwhelmed him and brought him down at last. And still his brave and loyal warriors stood as if rooted to the deck . . . staring at the glowing gray lamp of madness . . . motionless as stones, until the grinning, sardonic leader of the pirates, whom Karm Karvus now knew to be Red Kashtar himself, had spat out one ringing command:

"Kill!"

Then, as the grinning corsairs quitted the decks of the *Crown of Tsargol,* bearing away the Prince as their bound and helpless captive, the decks erupted into a gory battle. His soul twisting with revulsion, Karm Karvus had watched with horror as his men were transformed by that word into foaming, snarling beasts. Like mad dogs, the Tsargolians turned to rend one another with tooth and claw and naked strength, while the red corsairs of Tarakus laughed and made mock of them in their howling madness . . .

That had been many days ago. With a grim effort, Karm Karvus turned his memory from that nightmarish scene out of some scarlet pit of hell. *Father of Gods and Men—must I remember?*

The dungeon cell wherein they had hurled him was dark and clammy and foul with the stench of human droppings and the vile odor of rotten straw wherewith the bare, beslimed stone flags of the floor were strewn. From somewhere in the stone ceiling above, moisture dripped ceaselessly. The slow *plink-plunk* of it went on forever without change, and the monotony thereof drew his nerves taut and quivering.

His lips twisted in a wry smile. Little need had these sea wolves of Tarakus, to drive men mad with lamps of magic force: the dismal monotony of their foul and reeking dungeon cells were maddening enough.

The long hours of the day he passed in meditation. Betimes, to relieve the thick silence that was broken only by the ceaseless and maddening sound of dripping water, the captive Prince recited aloud in ringing tones such passages from the epics and sagas of his warlike people as he had aforetime committed to memory. And much thought he gave to the baffling problem of *why* he had been taken. At length he had come to the conclusion that the Red Brotherhood was grown ambitious and had dared to seek a mighty ransom from his city through threats to his captive person. His clear eyes went cold and bleak at the thought. His people loved him well, and well he knew how heavily they would pay to keep him safe from the burning needles and the tearing hooks of the torturers of Tarakus . . . and in his heart of hearts, Karm Karvus silently vowed that, if ever he escaped these black and loathsome pits and attained to freedom once again, he would not rest until he had burned this nest of robbers to the ground and hanged that sly and smirking rogue, their chieftain, from the gibbet.

Another possibility had occurred to him as well, and one by far the more daring and ambitious of the two. And that was that Kashtar the Red Wolf was grown avaricious beyond all conceivable cost of ransom of his person—and sought his very throne. Could it be that the corsair horde dared to seek to add scarlet-walled Tsargol to their pirate empire? It was not beyond the bounds of possibility. Karm Karvus prayed his nobles would be strong enough to seek to guard the greater good and keep their city free, even if it meant that by so doing they damned him to a slow and humiliating death under the knives of the torturers . . .

Thus he passed the slow, weary hours of his captivity, and waited for the opportunity to escape, if ever such should come. Nor did he ever guess the full magnitude of Kashtar's gigantic plot against the Six Cities . . .

*

AT last there came a break in the eternal monotony of his long imprisonment.

Karm Karvus had arisen from his troubled sleep and had put his hard body through the usual series of exercises, and had by now just completed the rude morning meal of sour wine and coarse bread and stale cheese. He was relaxing on his rough bunk, his mind busied with pondering the theorems of the old Lemurian philosopher, Tjanthon of Althaar, when he heard the thud of booted feet, the clank of weapons, and the jangling of accouterments approaching his place of captivity.

He sprang to full alertness on the instant. His gaolers

had, of course, disarmed him of all weaponry, but had as well left him unchained and in possession of the freedom of his cell. It was just barely possible that the men who now approached his door were few enough in number for his long-awaited attempt at escape. Perchance they expected to find him dull, bemused, languid from enforced lack of activity. If so, the wolves of Tarakus were in for a surprise. For, instead, they faced a clear-eyed fighting man in trim condition, and spoiling for battle.

There was the clatter of a key in the lock, then the groan of rusty hinges, and the door of the cell swung open. The glare of sputtering torches swept the cell with light—blinding light, to one who had spent many a day and night in utter blackness. His eyes slitted against the dazzle, Karm Karvus saw that seven guards stood at the entrance of to his cell, naked cutlasses in their hands. His face tightened grimly and his heart sank: they were taking no chances, and 'twould be an act of desperation to fling himself bare-handedly against such a number of armed and ready men.

The leader of the guards was a hard-faced man who would have been handsome in a sullen way had it not been for the sabre-cut that stretched his cheek from eye to jaw, and raised one lip in a perpetual snarl. He curtly commanded the Prince forth, and Karm Karvus stepped from his cell. The guards closed him in on all sides with naked steel.

They marched him through the dungeons, down rows of cells as vile and black as the one wherein he had passed so many dreary days and nights. Some were occupied and some were bare—and some, he saw, bore only gaunt skeletons, or raving, wide-eyed madmen, their reason crumbled from long years of hopeless prisonment.

At length they quitted the pits and rose through the levels of the rude palace of the pirate king. The surly lieutenant of the guards vouchsafed no explanation of why he had been taken from his cell, and, for his part, the proud young Prince of Tsargol disdained to ask. He strode briskly, his back erect as a spear-shaft, head held high, eyes fearless. Like a king he walked, and not a captive.

The palace of the Pirate City was a fantastic hovel filled with bemired and trampled splendors. Chests and casks of treasure were strewn carelessly about; rare tapestries and gorgeous silken hangings lay underfoot, muddy and torn. Goblets of exquisite worksmanship, statuettes of precious metal, artworks of rare ivory, scented woods, amber, crystal, jade and glistening onyx lay scattered about, broken and neglected, as if they were worthless trash.

As for the corsairs themselves, they were a motley lot, scum scraped from the gutters of a dozen cities. Filthy and bedraggled were they, unshaven and unshorn, but rings of bright gold bobbled in their earlobes or glittered on dirty fingers. Their garments had once been of princely finery, rare apricot satin and emerald velvet and glistening silks from Cadorna, all decked with rich lace and spun cloth-of-silver, gaudy with jeweled buttons or bespangled with priceless necklaces. But all this fine clothing was splattered with grease and mud and filthy with winestains. The pirate palace was filled with fabulous wealth, but here, it seemed, wealth had no particular value.

They came at last into the central hall of the main keep. Great candles as thick around as a man's thigh lit the scene of mired and neglected splendor. By the rich gold light, Karm Karvus could see a slim elegant man in red satin breeches and shirt, tight-stretched and close-fitting as a glove, who sprawled languidly atop the raised dais in a magnificent chair hewn from a single and tremendous ivory tusk. This man, sallow faced and silken-haired, slim fingers a-glitter with gems, was Kashtar, Lord of the Pirate City, Karm Karvus knew.

They regarded each other without words for a long moment. The pirate prince was slender and foppish and lazy as a great cat. His face was the smooth, glossy hue of old parchment and his eyes were cold black fire. The expression on his face was cruel, sardonic, sly. One great ruby like a hot coal smoldered at his lobe.

On a lower step of the dais stood another man whose peculiar garments caught the eye of Karm Karvus. He was tall and gaunt, his skull-like head shaven, his face coldly impassive, his eyes hooded and unreadable. He was robed in gray cloth in an unfamiliar, heiratic design, and curious glyphs in some unknown tongue were emblazoned on the breast of his robes in sullen crimson.

Karm Karvus knew this second man, as well. For this

could be none other than Kashtar's pet wizard, Belshathla, the evil genius of the pirate empire.

At length Kashtar smiled and made a mocking little half-bow. His voice was soft and there was laughter in it.

"Well, my lord Prince, I trust you have found your quarters suitable, and our hospitality pleasurable?"

"I have found your hospitality everything I had assumed it would be," replied Karm Karvus in calm, level tones.

"Excellent, excellent!" the pirate chieftain drawled. "I find myself overcome with boredom . . . my comrades and courtiers are, I fear, a rude and oafish lot, and hardly fit companions for a civilized man. I had hoped you might afford me some amusement."

"I thank you for that, but I must confess that I would much prefer the company of even such surly louts as your men, to a cold-blooded pig like yourself. I fear, sir, that you are not quite my notion of a civilized man."

Black fire flashed in the slitted eyes of the languid pirate leader and one slender hand stiffened, jeweled fingers curling about the glittering hilt of the longsword that hung at his thigh. For a moment he paled, then, and with an almost visible effort, he controlled the vicious flare of his temper. His voice fell to a silken purr.

"Splendid, splendid! You see, Belshathla, I knew our gallant princeling here could provide us with some amusement! Already, Prince, you begin to repay us for the hospitality we have lavished upon your comfort with so prodigal a hand."

The skull-faced wizard disdained to reply to his lord's pleasantry. Nor did Karm Karvus speak further. He stood, proudly silent, refusing to afford entertainment by any continued exchange. The cold malignant eyes of Kashtar surveyed him.

"Doubtless, my lord Prince, you have occupied your time under our roof with some little speculation as to our reasons for making you our guest, and the ultimate purposes to which we intend putting your presence here among us, eh?"

"Not really," said Karm Karvus levelly. "Does the helpless animal wonder at being locked in a pig-sty? Doubtless, it is to be fattened for the slaughter. In my case, I am immured in your pig-sty of a palace for ransom, I doubt me not—since you are nothing but a common criminal."

Again his measured words stung Kashtar almost to the brink of fury. A dark flush stained his lean and sallow cheeks and rage glittered in his hard cold eyes. And, again, he mastered his temper with an iron control.

"Harsh words—harsh words, for one completely in my power!" he purred, and there was the note of silken menace in his tones.

"You can but kill me," Karm Karvus shrugged. Then, quoting the familiar words of his old comrade, Thongor, he added: "And a man may die but once, when all is said."

Rather to his surprise, the Prince of Tarakus laughed.

" 'Ransom'—I fear you mistake me for a common bandit! And 'kill'—again you mistake me, Tsargolian!"

"For a common butcher, perhaps?" the prisoner suggested. Eyes of cold black fire narrowed.

"No, no, my pretty prince, I reserve you for no such fate! Instead, a higher purpose requires you as my—ah—my guest," he drawled. Karm Karvus shook himself impatiently.

"Come, name the price of my freedom, and have done with this cat-and-mouse game," he said. "Whatever your fee, my people will raise it."

"But your freedom has no price on it," the Red Wolf smiled suavely; "or, at least, no price your own small monarchy can afford. But the high and mighty Thongor, now . . . ah yes, he can well pay the price . . ."

Now it was the turn of the captive to feel the flick of stinging words. A ghost of apprehension moved in the eyes of Karm Karvus.

"Thongor? What has he to do with all this?" he demanded.

"Nothing, as yet, but soon—soon!" chuckled the pirate chieftain. "Soon he will pay the price, and a dear one 'twill be, by the Eleven Scarlet Hells!"

"I do not—understand?"

"Then I shall be pleased to explain." Kashtar leaned forward, resting his elbow on the arms of his carven ivory seat and regarding Karm Karvus intently.

"You are an old friend of the Lord of Patanga," he

purred. "And I doubt me not, he feels towards you with a warmth of friendship almost worthy of our demands—but not quite. *But*—when we have in some little measure *added* to our little collection of the friends of the so-called Lord of the West—"

"*Added?*" demanded Karm Karvus, hoarsely.

"Aye! Now let me see; there is the Prince Ald Turmis of the city of Shembis, and old Barand Thon, lord of Thurdis of the Dragon, and the young Prince Zul who but last year succeeded his elder brother to the throne of Zangabal, and—"

Perspiration burst out on the brows of Karm Karvus.

"What—what deviltry *is* this?" he groaned.

Kashtar's face broke into a gloating grin, and he drew himself up in a lordly posture. "Why, with the reigning monarchs of five of the six cities of his empire under our thumb, this upstart Barbarian cannot refuse to deliver all of Patanga city into our hands, and thus in one blow the pirates of Tarakus have seized the greatest prize on earth—*the Empire itself*. And should perchance the Barbarian decide to fight for his throne, you and your fellow princelings will die under the knives—and we shall sweep the walls of Patanga with that same deathly ray of madness wherewith we whelmed your ship. Aye, my pretty Prince, this time mere ransom of gold or gems will not feed our hunger . . . this time 'tis crowns we crave. And we shall have them, or else plunge half a world under the Gray Death!"

Frozen with astonishment and horror, Karm Karvus could think of nothing to say. Was it his terrible fate to be used as a tool to draw Thongor and all his people under the grim hand of slavery to the cruel and treacherous pirates of Tarakus?

Alas, so it would seem.

CHAPTER 6:

DARK WISDOM FROM EARTH'S DAWN

They took him down to a black sea cave
That under the fortress lay,
And there on the breast of a mighty wave,
A dragon roared at bay—

—The Tsargol Records

KARM KARVUS woke slowly. He was dazed, his mind a blur, and for a long moment he did not know where he was nor what had chanced.

His interrogation before the ivory throne of Kashtar Red Wolf was long over. After the devastating revelation that, through him, a great danger was to threaten the empire of Thongor the Mighty, he had been returned to his cell at mid-day. The rest of the afternoon had been passed in self-recrimination and despair. Then the evening meal had been brought to him. Usually, it was a drab affair, but this evening there was a jug of good wine. He had drunk deep, and thereafter an unwonted sleepiness had come over him, and the Prince of Tsargol had stretched out on his crude bunk and slept heavily. Slept, to awaken—*where?*

He lay on a soft couch spread with many small bright pillows and a rich, silken spread of Zangabali work. Looking around, he saw he lay in a chamber of dressed stone, well lit with many small hanging lamps of pierced brass. In a corner, on a low tabouret of black wood set with mother-of-pearl, a huge thurible of massy silver smoked. Blue fumes of incense trickled from it to fill the room with the rich odor of nard and myrrh.

Hangings adorned the wall and they pictured forth incredible visions, subtly pornographic. On a long low table of hewn and polished marble stood a statue of wrought gold which depicted a young girl copulating with three satyrs. Karm Karvus shook his head and closed his eyes; his brain felt numb and his body was lax with a strange weakness. The odor of the incense was overpoweringly sweet.

"Drug . . . something in the wine . . ."

"Correct, Prince of Tsargol," a harsh, grating voice said.

His eyes snapped open and he looked around. There was a huge chair of mellow golden wood drawn up against the further wall; it was carven all over with leering devil-masks and monstrous faces, and these faces were busy at innumerable disgusting and erotic tasks. He tore his eye from the obscene carvings and looked up at the tall gaunt man with the shaven skull-like face who sat therein, wrapped in hieratic robes of neutral gray.

"Belshathla? What—"

He strove to rise to his feet, but a wave of nausea went through him and he sank back limply. The Gray Magician nodded, thin lips spread in a mirthless grin.

"Aye, Belshathla . . . the weakness will soon pass, Prince, and you will be yourself again," the other grated.

"But why . . ."

"The drug in your wine? 'Twas nothing—a pinch of Rose-of-Dreams, no more. More would have plunged you in a sleep so deep that death itself would not awaken you . . . and I wanted you *alive!*"

There was a grim, merciless glee in the rasping tones of the other's voice. Karm Karvus could not understand what was happening, nor where he was, nor how he had come to this strange place, with its vile decorations and over-sweet air. He put his hand to his throbbing head and strove to clear his wits.

"I know the questions that roil and seethe within you, and it pleases me to answer them," Belshathla continued in his harsh, metallic voice. "I had you drugged and brought here by my servitors, because I wished to look upon you in your helplessness . . . doubtless, my noble lord, you will not recall the incident, but seven years ago I visited your court in Tsargol city as a lowly petitioner . . . but perchance you *do* remember the event?"

Karm Karvus shook his head numbly.

" 'Twas a year or so before the lord Thongor went up against Black Zaar . . . no? Ah, well, doubtless I was too lowly and unimportant for one of your exalted rank to bother with remembering," Belshathla harshed. His tones were bitter and sardonic; doubtless his failure at the court of Tsargol had rankled greatly, souring his pride. Karm Karvus strove to recall the incident, but failed.

"I had, through lonely years of patient toil, rediscovered in old charts the location of the lost cities of Nianga in the days of its greatness and power . . . and, for that I did dwell in the Scarlet City by the Sea, I came first to your court, offering you vast wealth and power and unconquerable strength in war, if you would from your bulging coffers advance the funds wherewith to purchase an expedition to the drear and barren wastelands of Nianga. But you, my gracious lord, said I was mad, and had me driven forth from your palace . . . ah! I see that at last you have remembered!"

Karm Karvus turned a bleak gaze on the man in gray.

"Yes," he said slowly, "I do indeed remember you now, although you called yourself by another name and affected the white robes of a scholarly Nephelos in those days, instead of the gray raiment of the Niangan sorcerers. As I recall, I said you were mad to wish to bring to light again the devil-magic of Nianga . . . that the Gods in their infinite wisdom had crushed all of that accursed realm into ruin, so that the contagion of that evil science might not spread like some terrible and deadly plague across Lemuria. I said also that it was better for Mankind that the devil-machines of darkling Nianga lie forever beneath the dust of the ages and never be brought to the light of day again . . . yes, I remember the incident well!"

The thin lips of the Gray Magician writhed in a vulpine leer of gloating triumph. "I thought I might refresh your memory, my hapless Prince! I fled the gates of Tsargol with curses on my lips, and in my righteous anger I swore that I should recover the lost wisdom of aeon-dead Nianga without your aid, and that when I had mastered the mighty engines of destruction I hoped to find amongst the ruins, it should be Tsargol the Scarlet that should first groan under the lash of my revenge . . . aye, for years I labored alone amidst the deathly wastes of that drear and accursed land, and with these two hands I dug away the dust of ages and brought the great engines to the light of day again. And then followed more years of terrible, grueling labor as I learned the forgotten sciences of Earth's Dawn and one by one the dark wisdoms of age-lost and legended Nianga became mine . . ."

Maniacal triumph rang in the hoarse voice of the Gray Magician as he ranted. A mad glare lit his cold eyes and whitish foam bedrabbled the corners of his mouth. And Karm Karvus saw that the man was indeed mad: whether he had been mad, years before, when first he brought his blasphemous proposal to the foot of the Scarlet Throne, none could say; perhaps the long lonely years of backbreaking toil had taken their toll of his tottering sanity, or the long brooding on the fancied rebuff . . . but wherever that fine and brilliant mind had cracked, cracked it had, and the man before him now was a raving madman. Karm Karvus thought swiftly. Perhaps he could play on the other's delusions of persecution and yearnings for power and revenge, and find therein a method of escape.

"I was a fool to ever doubt your genius, O Belshathla," the Prince said firmly, and there was the ring of sincerity in his voice. A flush of triumph darkened the gaunt cheeks of the Gray Magician and he laughed triumphantly.

"Now you bemoan your short-sightedness, now, O Prince, that it is too late! Once I could have laid the kingdoms of the earth at your feet, but, ah, now I have offered them to this red dog of Tarakus . . . 'tis he, not you, shall rule from the throne-of-thrones!"

"Alas, then, for my failure to recognize a powerful intellect when it came before me," Karm Karvus said. "But—have you *really* mastered the long-dead sciences of Nianga—or do you but make pretence, to gain revenge?"

"Pretence?" Rage blazed up in the glittering eyes of Belshathla. "Pretence, is it? I, the last of the Gray Magicians of Nianga—a *pretender?* I, before whose wisdom the kingdoms of the world shall bow down—I, who shall be hailed as lord and conqueror, when I take my place upon the throne of the mightiest empire the earth has ever known? Listen to me, my petty princeling: the Gray Death, as you in your ignorance may call the Mind-Distorting Lamp, is but the least and littlest of all the terrible weapons in the mighty arsenals of God-whelmed and age-forgot Nianga! There is a weapon in those buried crypts that can unleash the very fury of the Sun itself, and touch a flame so furious that the solid earth itself is made to melt and run like spring ice before the hot white dawn . . . aye, Thunder's Egg, the wise men of old Nianga called it . . . two rare and precious metals, when brought together in unguarded proximity, work such a magic 'twixt themselves that the blazing fury of the Sun itself, which sleeps ensorcelled in all solid matter, roars up in a colossal pillar of seething flame, towering over the groaning earth like a flaming tree, rooted deep in the everlasting fires of hell!"

Karm Karvus, with what inward horror I give my readers leave to picture for themselves, listened as mad Belshathla raved and ranted on. The Prince of Tsargol, of course, had never before heard of a hydrolithium bomb, but such it was that the Gray Magician sought to describe for him, although he lacked a terminology and was forced to employ the euphemisms of magic.

The young Prince let the madman bluster on until he thought the fellow had exhausted his lust for triumphant gloating; then, and humbly, as a lowly student begging for a display of the Master's lore, he suggested that he would like to see the Lamp of Madness in full use. To this the Gray Magician made swift and eager assent: nothing delighted him more than to flaunt his science before the humble admiration of one who had once spurned it.

He rose and thrust aside a hanging, revealing the black mouth of a hidden passage. Commanding Karm Karvus to attend, he led the way, lighting the black tunnel with a flickering candelabra. Karm Karvus followed closely at his heels, mind working furiously. He was unbound and no guards or servitors were in sight. He could well strike down the madman now, and take to his heels . . . but he knew not in what portion of the palace they were, nor how to escape therefrom, so he decided to let the madman lead him further, and await a better opportunity.

Thus he followed the gaunt figure of the mad magician into the blackness of the tunnel, knowing not where it might lead him, but trusting to his Gods.

*

THEY went down a coiling stone stair that lined the inner throat of a mighty shaft. Down, down, deep within the earth they descended, until it seemed to Karm Karvus that a heavy mountain of stone pressed down upon the darkness. The city of Tarakus was builded in a half-circle around the bay, and tier on tier of houses rose up the slopes of the steep and rocky promontory that thrust out into the wide waste of waters where the mighty Gulf of Patanga mingled with the thunderous waves of the Southern Sea. The citadel of Kashtar was itself built upon the heights, and this secret stair, it seemed, descended deep below the city . . . perhaps to sea level.

He followed the shuffling sandals of the magician through the echoing darkness. It was a thrilling and an eerie scene . . . the wavering candlelight, the gaunt robed figure, the walls of naked rock that lifted about them as they descended deeper and ever deeper into the nameless abyss of darkness.

They emerged at length into a tremendous natural cavern, like the domed hall of some primitive cathedral. Hundreds of feet above their heads, an arched roof soared, dangling stone stalactites lost in thickly-clotted shadows.

Karm Karvus looked down and saw, far below, the waters of the sea pounding against sharp rocks. Peering through the gloom, he could faintly perceive an arched opening in the further wall of the cavern, through which the waves entered. Oddly, a mighty grille of steel bars closed that cavernous mouth. Karm Karvus could discern no reason for so curious a barrier, but he shelved the question until another time.

They stood on a deep ledge and near the place whereat they were, a jutting spar of heavy rock thrust out over the thunderous chasm. A glittering structure of crystal globes and rods of twinkling brass had been erected at the end of this jutting spar. It was the very twin of the hellish instrument that had struck terror, madness and death into the hearts of the crewmen of the *Crown of Tsargol*.

Belshathla followed the Prince's glance, and burst into harsh, cackling laughter.

"Aye, the Mind-Distorting Lamp . . . the Ray of Madness itself . . . the only other existing copy of the instrument mounted aboard our Kashtar's own flagship, the *Red Wolf*," he grated. Then, gesturing around, he said:

"This is my laboratorium, and here I conduct my experiments far from the spying eyes and ears of jealous men."

"Here?" queried Karm Karvus in surprise. "You experiment here? But on—*what?*"

Belshathla shrugged. "Slaves mostly. See you those hanging cages?"

Karm Karvus had not seen them before in the dim light, but now he followed the pointing finger of the mad magician and his gorge rose in nausea at what his eyes gazed upon.

A dozen cages of rusty iron dangled by chains from the groined ceiling of the cavern far above. There were dead men, and women, too, and some there were that had not died—whimpering, wild-eyed things that mouthed and mewled and slavered. *The mad!*

"Most of *those* experiments are finished with," confided Belshathla. "And when they are no longer of any use to my scientific research, I dispose of them—thusly!" He reached out and caressed a great lever with the palm of one claw-like hand. Karm Karvus saw that the catch of the lever released sprockets in the bottom grille of each cage in numbered sequence. When the mad scientist was finished with the poor wretches, he could tip them screaming into the sea far below. And then it was that Karm Karvus saw the reason for the barred entrance . . .

A heavy reptilian head came rushing up from the floor of the cavern, the waves breaking on its blunt, wedge-shapen skull, cold eyes flaming with ophidian hunger. Belshathla had somehow trapped in his cavern one of the mighty sea dragons of the Lemurian deeps. And, suddenly, the hazy outlines of an idea arose in the quick mind of Karm Karvus.

He assumed a critical, almost contemptuous expression. Surveying the pitiful, whimpering things in the cages, he said dubiously: "These creatures are all dead—dead, or already mad. How can I see the weapon of your genius in its full power, with such poor mewling subjects? Can you use the ray on—*that?*"

He pointed below them, at the tremendous dragon of the abyss. A touch of fear came into the face of the mad magician.

"Why, I—I do not—*yes,* of course!" Belshathla

blustered. He busied himself with the weird glittering machine. A deep-throated humming awoke within the hellish instrument. Strange lights glowed and flashed, and the stench of nameless chemicals came harsh and hot to his nostrils. Karm Karvus held his breath in anticipation. He had but the vaguest idea of what was going to happen—his plans were rudimentary in the extreme—but somehow, letting one incident lead to another, he thought he saw a way out of this predicament. If he could destroy both Belshathla and the Ray of Madness, that would leave but the duplicate instrument mounted on the bows of the corsair flagship—it seemed worth a try!

Belshathla was ready for the monstrous experiment. Cold lights gleamed up from the raygun, transforming his face into a weird mask of highlights and shadows.

"Be careful not to look full into the ray," he cautioned, "but turn your gaze away. First, I will use the beam at the lowest settings—watch!"

The humming sound rose to a maddening whine. Now. from the central globe, a throbbing beam of completely colorless light shone. The cold finger of pallid luminance glowed faintly through the echoing gloom. It stretched from the rocky prominence whereon they stood, probing down into the watery abyss—to bathe the lifted head of the monster reptile full in its flickering beam!

Slowly, the eyes of the dragon blinked sleepily—glazed—and became motionless, riveted upon the source of the colorless ray. The dragon lay, half submerged, rapt: the Lamp of Madness held its mind locked.

"This," said Belshathla conversationally, "is the same setting to which the instrument was attuned when we took your vessel. If you will recall, your men were completely hypnotized, enthralled, frozen, their attention fixed upon the ray. In this state, the mind is completely under the dominance of whomever controls the Lamp, and will take any suggestion given it. Your men were transformed from motionless statues to roaring, battling madmen when Kashtar commanded them to kill, you may recall. Of course, the dragon cannot be so commanded, as, a mere beast, it does not understand spoken commands. But if I increase the vibratory level of the ray, and build its intensity, it will go wild—behold!"

He made some adjustment to the whirling crystal globes, and even as he spoke, the burning eyes of the monster reptile flared crimson and it gave voice to a thunderous bellow of maniacal frenzy. The great lash of its tail whipped the cold black waters to fury in an explosion of flying white foam.

Karm Karvus had been playing this scene by pure instinct, not at all certain where it would lead. Now he suddenly saw—and sprang back as the mighty larth, bellowing in its mad fury, came clashing and scrabbling up against the cliffy wall of rock, which shuddered under the impact of its colossal weight. The ledge shook—black cracks shot forth in sudden zigzags—rock crumpled, splintered, gave way.

Now Belshathla recoiled, white-faced and shaken. The smooth and sceptical words of the Tsargolian had subtly led him on; but now, seeing what he had wrought, the Gray Magician feared for the safety of his instrument—and his person. But it was too late. With a grinding roar, the ledge broke away, and fell. The Lamp of Madness went twinkling down through the foam and spray and was lost. Karm Karvus felt a pang of fierce joy go through him—now the pirates of Tarakus had only one other such weapon wherewith to imperil the Empire!

The next moment, his joy vanished, for he himself was falling. Black water and white foam and the enraged, thrashing sea monster swung up towards him as he fell amidst a cloud of broken rock into the chaos of waters far below.

Belshathla alone did not fall: he managed to seize hold of the rocky cliff and sustain himself even as the ledge collapsed. Shaken and gasping, he dragged himself back into the mouth of the tunnel. Through his pride and folly, the irreplaceable second Lamp had been lost, and with it Kashtar's precious captive, the Prince of Tsargol.

For surely nothing could survive in that thundering maelstrom of battering waves and shattering spray . . .

CHAPTER 7:

THE FACE AT THE WINDOW

The stars are bright, the wind is cold,
The moon is drifting free.
We're out to seek for pirate gold
Across a silver sea.

—Sea Chantey of the Pirates of Tarakus

SUNSET flared crimson in the west, and a scudding wrack of wind-torn clouds gave ominous presage of coming storms. Below, the long rocky promontory thrust forth from the southernmost tip of Ptartha into the great waste of waters where the Patangan Gulf joined the limitless reaches of Yashengzeb Chun.

Tarakus the Pirate City was builded on the uttermost tip of this savage mass of wet black rock, where curved breakwaters formed a quiet harbor. Thunderous waves crashed against this sea-wall in blinding sheets of flying spray and seething foam. But above, the city of the corsairs climbed in rising tiers above the stormy main.

The Pirate City resembled a fortress. Soaring, square-sided stone towers rose against the flame of sunset. Beetling walls and heavily-manchicolated battlements stood about the city like sheltering arms. High above the city, on the upmost slopes of the black promontory, the massive stone citadel of Kashtar brooded down upon his domain.

In the harbor below, more than one hundred vessels rode at anchor. Dragon-prowed galleys and high-pooped ships of war, lean caravels and stout carracks—the mightiest armada of all the World's West was moored below the corsair capitol. But rarely did so many of the Captains of the Coast bring their savage, black-hulled sea wolves home to anchorage at the same time. But now were they launched on the mightiest expedition of all time—the invasion and conquest of an empire. And even now the harbor was a bustling scene of furious industry, as stores and provisions were shipped aboard and vessels were set in fighting trim for the great war against Patanga, the City of the Flame.

Kashtar the Red Wolf was in a howling rage. The loss of Karm Karvus, and the destruction of the second instrument, had goaded him to fury. For his plans had long been set and were now thrown into confusion by this unexpected event. It had been his cunning scheme to seize upon other of the Lords of the Empire, even as he had captured the Prince of Tsargol, and to use these valued friends of Thongor as hostages. But this would take months—and had he time to spare? Was Karm Karvus dead, or had he perchance escaped alive from the subterranean cavern? Cold reason and logic said that there was little chance of one man escaping with his life from the seething inferno of thundering water, wherein a maddened larth writhed in wild convulsions. But reason and logic were not enough—were Karm Karvus to escape, and were he to carry the alarm to Patanga, Tarakus would lose all element of precious surprise, and would face an alert and ready opponent when at last the great corsair armada sailed into the harbor of Patanga.

Thus was the fleet being brought to sudden readiness. And, as well, Kashtar's men were combing the city for any slightest token of Karm Karvus.

Alert corsairs strode about the harbor, the rocks, the seawall, beaming bright lanterns and flickering torches into dark places. Mounted on swift-striding kroters, parties of well-armed pirates rode the crowded streets and about the outer walls of the city, searching for any sign of the escaped captive.

The city itself was ablaze under the crimson skies, for the crews of a hundred ships were in port. Every ale house and wineshop and inn was filled with rough-voiced, swaggering seamen roaring for drink and food and women.

Wineshop signs swung on creaking hinges in the gusts of salty wind. Drunken song and the roar of revelry thundered up against the elemental fury of the storm. For now the howling gale was broke and sleety rains swept the twisting, cobbled ways. Staggering celebrants lurched into inn and ale shop for shelter against the downpour, but the keen-eyed, hard-faced guard parties merely wrapped their sea cloaks about themselves and grimly strode on. Every street and square, every hovel and house would be searched that night on orders from Red Kashtar. If Karm Karvus was abroad in the city—he would be found.

Hour after hour, as the storm raged and thunder went bellowing down the sky, they searched on. Lightning flared and flickered amid boiling black clouds; icy rains sluiced the cobbled alleys; but the search went on.

*

WHILE the guards of Tarakus scoured the streets and buildings of the Pirate City for any trace of Karm Karvus, the fugitive himself had taken refuge in the one place most likely to be overlooked by even the most cunning and doggedly determined of the searchers.

In short, he was upon the roofs.

The Tsargolian never quite knew how he had survived the weltering fury of torn black water wherein the dragon, goaded beyond endurance, floundered and squalled. Somehow, after an eternity of swimming blind through black cold water far under the surface—lungs near to bursting and red agony searing at his brain—he had come up, gasping and half-drowned, in the fetid air of the sewers.

The pirates of Tarakus were not a cleanly lot, but when a city is constructed upon the slopes of a rocky ridge honeycombed with subterranean lakes and river-channels, it is an easy and obvious thing to build a sewer system. And it was the luck of the Gods that led the Prince, lost in the darkness, to emerge in one of the sewer tunnels.

From thence he had clambered up into the streets of the city. By yet a second stroke of good fortune, the narrow alley was dark and deserted at this hour. With a heave of strong shoulders, the Prince shoved the rusty grating aside, and crawled out—muddy, bedraggled, smeared with filthy garbage from head to foot—but alive. And, for the moment, safe.

But for how long?

He prowled the little-used side streets, keeping well in the shadows, and for a time he sought to find a way out of the city. Once beyond the walls, he could make his way down the length of the rocky promontory, rejoin the mainland, and trust to his luck in the jungles of Ptartha. He might be able to find friendly fishermen in some jungle cove, and thus gain transportation to the nearest city of the Empire. That he could worry about later, when the time came. His first problem was to find some way of leaving the Pirate City unobserved.

He took the only route to safety that occurred to him—the rooftops. There, in the windswept darkness, well above lighted doorways and swinging lanterns, high above blazing windows, guttering torches, or the eyes of passers-by, lost in the black confusion of roofs and domes, chimneys and gables, he hoped to elude detection.

And thus far the ruse had worked. The streets of Tarakus were narrow and the houses were set very close together. It was not a difficult matter to clamber or to leap from one rooftop to another, and he found it comparatively easy to make progress across the city. On a clear and a fair night, he might have been spotted more easily—a black figure moving against the bright tropic stars. But amidst howling gusts of sleety rain, only fools peer skyward with open eyes. And, as well, on a clear night of no storms, the clatter and thump of his boots on the roof-tiles might well have been heard by those within. Luckily, this night was a loud and stormy one, and no one heard—or if they did hear his passage, they did not bother to give it a second thought.

But the breaking of the storm, which had long impended, proved in itself a hazard. It is difficult enough to clamber across tilted roofs and slippery tiles, but to do so in streaming rain, with howling gusts of wind to knock you off balance and tear loose your fingerholds, is another and much more difficult matter. After several near slips, Karm Karvus determined that, whatever the hazard, he was going to have to seek a haven somewhere—and soon. One incautious step—one slip of his footing—and he would end up with a broken leg or a cracked skull on the wet glistening cobbles below.

Some of the houses had two and even three storeys, although by far the greater number were low-roofed one-storey buildings. It seemed to Karm Karvus that he would have a much greater chance to hide in safety and elude detection, if he entered the upper storey of some large building. At length a choice window came to his view.

Most of the upper windows were either tightly shuttered and locked, or securely barred with cold iron. But this one, although shuttered, was open. Indeed, it was the creak and slap of the unfastened shutter that first drew his attentions to it.

In a city filled with pirates, it would seem obvious to expect an occasional thief. But the roof wherein this window was set was high and very steep, and it lifted well above the level of its nearest neighbors—hence, it would seem, the owners thereof were somewhat careless about fastening it. For what thief would be so foolish as to risk a broken neck striving to gain its sill?

Karm Karvus was no fool, but he was a desperate man—and the extremities of desperation are sometimes but a hair's-breadth away from foolhardiness. So he climbed the roof.

He fumbled and fought for handholds with fingers numb from the cold rain and raw from rough stone and broken tiles. Three times he almost slipped and fell—and three times desperation sent a jolt of new strength surging through his exhausted body, and he caught another hold. Foot by foot, up the steep incline of slippery tiles—streaming all the while with cold rain—he inched his way to the haven of the open and unlit window. He could hardly see from the stinging rain beating at his eyes. His arms, shoulders and back were bone-weary from the strain. The icy, insubstantial fingers of the howling stormwind plucked and tore at him, striving to claw him free from his slight fingerholds and pitch him over into the dark alley far below.

But Karm Karvus had iron self-control and infinite patience. Grimly setting his jaw and ignoring the ache in his exhausted muscles, the numbness in his cold fingers, he struggled on, foot by foot. And in time he reached the peaked spine of the roof.

Here the footing was easier. A shallow gutter ran along the peak of the roof, and it was possible to stand erect by straddling this gutter. Thus he made more rapid progress, with surer footing, the length of the roof up to the very sill of the window.

And the lights went on.

The Prince froze motionless as a horn lantern flared up behind the rain-drenched panes.

Peering in, he saw a veiled figure near the window, the lantern in its hand. A face peered out at him—a pale, blurred oval. Man or woman? Friend or foe? The Prince of Tsargol could not guess—neither could he delay. In the rainy darkness he had been careless of discovery. Here, on the peak of the roof, his body bathed in lantern-light, he could clearly be seen from the street below or from the window of a near house, if anyone happened to be looking.

Taking a deep breath, and acutely unconscious that he had nothing but his bare hands wherewith to fight, he smashed one booted foot against the diamond panes and came crashing into the room.

Before the veiled figure could move or speak, Karm Karvus had grasped it in powerful hands. One forearm was clamped across his captive's throat—perhaps he should break his captive's neck now, before it had a chance to cry out and give the alarm—

CHAPTER 8:

RIVER OF TERROR

This is the song that the Jungle sings,
Of dark green gloom where the bright vine swings,
And the scarlet parrots squawk and screech
And green bamboos line the sun-burnt beach;
Of yellow sky and the tangled brush
And the breathless speed of a vandar's rush,
Where jungle blossoms are burning red
And blood-vines sway to the wild zamph's tread;
O these are the sights that the Jungle brings,
And this is the song that the Jungle sings.

—Drum-Song of the Kodanga Tribesmen

FOR a long time he lay face-down in the wet gray sand, a sodden bundle, lacking the strength to rise.

For longer than he ever guessed, Thongor of Valkarth had fought his way through the waves. The surging undertow had torn him loose from his perilous perch astride the neck of the sea dragon many minutes after the monster had submerged; The currents had carried them apart and he had not again encountered it. Whether his swordblows had dealt the larth a killing wound or whether it had survived, he was never to know. But when his brawny shoulders clove the surface of the gulf once again, the *Scimitar* was no longer in sight.

And he was alone and lost amidst the blue waters. For a time, the Barbarian tread water, peering about for some sign of the pirate galley. His undersea battle with the sea dragon had, it seemed, carried him farther away from the ship than he could have guessed. But there was no point in worrying about that. Safety—the nearest shore—lay directly east. And so he turned into the dawn and began to swim.

Now he lay, battered and breathless and weary, in the clinging sands. Somehow he had accomplished the incredible task. Bone-deep exhaustion had robbed his limbs of all feeling and of all strength—but he had come ashore and now he could rest. For a time he slept, a deep dreamless sleep of utter exhaustion.

When he awoke, it was nearly sundown. His arms and shoulders ached with weariness, his throat was raw from salt water, but the yawning void in his middle clamored to be filled. Staggering to his feet, Thongor headed for the jungle and in an instant the green foliage had swallowed him from view.

Within the rustling green twilight he stood motionless for a few moments, gazing about. He stood in a murmuring world of shadows and mystery. Thick leaves and long grasses lay underfoot, and the rank odor of rotting vegetation, leaf mold, and the heady perfume of jungle blossoms rose to his nostrils. All about him, in the mystic emerald hush, the purple or scarlet boles of great trees rose like columns in some weird cathedral. Overhead, a matted tangle of interwoven boughs and thick leaves formed a domelike canopy of foliage through which only a few dim sunbeams found passage, to splatter the jungle floor with hot gold.

Strange blossoms blazed, clots of vivid color against glossy green-black leaves. Dangling vines hung like somnolent and sluggish serpents in the deep jade gloom. Thongor drew his mighty broadsword with a rasp of steel on leather, as he began to explore. This fantastic realm of bizarre and incredible beauty was, he knew, haunted by shapes of death and terror. Those branches far above his head might conceal the sliding coils of the dread oph, the great horned serpent of the Lemurian jungles, whose blade-ridged spine could slash manflesh to ribbons and whose pallid and glistening length could lash about a warrior and crush his limbs to pulp in instants.

Here, too, dwelt the photh, the scarlet vampire bat who was one of the terrors of the jungle. But the denizens of Ptartha most to be feared were the titanic predators, the colossal jungle dragon whose insatiable hunger made its entire life one unceasing hunt for red meat; or the kingly vandar, the jungle lion, many times larger and much more ferocious than his modern-day descendants. As well, the fierce zulphar, the massive wild Lemurian boar, might well be hidden behind any bush. And the shadows of that thicket ahead could well be the haunt of the dread deodath, the terrible dragon-cat whose mad ferocity and savage strength made its name a legend of fear . . .

His bow and quiver had been lost in his long battle amidst the waves, but he had had the presence of mind to thrust his mighty broadsword back into the scabbard that hung at his girdle, and so he was still armed. He must hunt swiftly, in order to make a kill before darkness rendered it impossible. Luckily, he found game almost immediately—a plump phondle at a waterhole. His sword was too cumbersome for this kind of work, but a slim dirk was scabbarded at his side. The swift, hurtling glitter of the thrown blade flashed momently in the dim green twilight of the jungle clearing, and its bright flash was quenched in the hot scarlet of the phondle's blood. The fat, gazelle-like little grass-eater went down kicking, and Thongor had meat.

He made a fire from dry leaves and deadwood, painstakingly scraping the steel dagger-blade against a flinty rock until the sparks caught. Hacking off one plump phondle haunch, he roasted it over the crackling fire and gorged himself on the delicious steak. When he was finished with his meal, he drank long and deeply of the pure cold waters of the waterhole, washing the blood from his hands.

Thongor was not native to these jungle coasts, but he had long since mastered the arts of survival in the green tropical brush. Once, scarce more than a boy, he had crossed a thousand leagues of the jungles of Chush on foot and alone—and he had learned to survive. That had been when he first crossed the Mountains of Mommur, leaving his frigid homeland in the North far behind, gambling his future on the glittering barbaric cities of the jungled South. He had lived. And he had learned his lessons well.

A distant, coughing roar came to his alert ears. The jungles of Ptartha are no different from the jungles of Chush, and the sound of a hunting vandar—the great black-maned lion of ancient Lemuria—is instantly recognizable as the sound of a hunting vandar. His fires were now glowing coals: he could have built a roaring blaze again, but thought to find a safer haven aloft in the trees. For the mighty vandar of the Lemurian jungle is not a tree-cat, unlike his distant cousin, the dreaded sabretooth.

He spent that night in the crotch of a towering jungle monarch, and woke with dawn refreshed, rested, his strength renewed. Descending from his high branch, he found the remains of last night's kill gone. A grim smile touched his stern lips. The vandar, too, had gone to his rest with a full belly!

To break his fast on lush tropical fruits and berries was no problem. His problem lay in what he should do next. He knew not where he had come ashore, nor how distant the nearest city might lay. Zangabal was doubtless too far away; Pelorm might be much nearer, but Thongor did not know whether he had come to shore above or below that city. For all he knew, the waves had carried him further south than seemed likely, and he was only a league or so above the rocky promontory whereon was builded Tarakus. Nor, in this dense jungle, was he likely to find a landmark that would tell him his location.

But in his early years, long ere he had risen to the throne of Patanga, when the young Thongor had brawled and battled his way through half the cities of the West as bandit chieftain, mercenary sword, wandering thief and pirate captain, he had known these jungles well. Indeed, his bandit days had carried him far through these very jungles—in the days ere he had been captured and chained to the galleys of Shembis, from whence he had escaped to join the corsairs. Mayhap he would indeed come across some sign or landmark whereby he might recognize his location.

But first he must have weapons. One does not fight the monster predators of the Ptarthan jungles, armed only with a sword and a dirk. The weapons of choice are hunting spear and longbow. It was probably beyond his powers to fashion a good hunting bow, for lack of seasoned wood and the proper materials from which to devise a taut bowstring, to say nothing of the difficulties involved in making well-balanced and barbed arrows. But a spear, or at least a javelin, he could indeed make, and did.

A few hours later, with a rough quiver of five short javelins strapped to his shoulders, Thongor started off through the jungles. In lieu of steel-bladed tips for the light throwing spears, he had sharpened them with his dirk and then hardened the tips in the coals of his fire, an old trick he had once learned from the Rmoahal hordesmen of the distant Eastern plains.

By early afternoon, he reached the shores of a rushing river. This, he assumed—and correctly, as it turned out—was Amadon, the Jungle River. At least, he knew of no other river of this size in all this portion of the Ptarthan jungles. And if this was Amadon, finding it was a stroke of genuine luck. For this powerful current could carry him almost to the gates of Tarakus, since the Amadon clove its watery way through the Southern jungles, its mouth lying not far from the walls of Tarakus.

He set about building a rude raft. The fallen logs that lay nearby were deeply buried in dead leaves and had rotted, the most of them, beyond possibility of use. But the raw materials of such a raft as he envisioned grew all about him in the form of half-grown young saplings. With the keen blade of his great broadsword, Sarkozan, and the strength of his mighty thews, he felled the young trees and wove them together with springy, tough lianas. The raft was small and light and rather flimsy, but Thongor thought it would suffice.

He set forth on the rushing current, keeping clear of the banks and of occasional snags by means of a long pole he had also cut. The foaming water rushed along, and Thongor grinned with satisfaction. Soon he was making many times the speed he would otherwise have made had he attempted to slog along through the dense underbrush afoot.

*

TOWARD twilight—terror struck!

Poling a clear passage through the gushing waters, Thongor felt a sudden weight land on his shoulders and the sharp sting of fangs cutting his flesh. Had he not been standing with legs spread and knees slightly bent to keep his balance on the wobbling raft, he might well have been knocked off his feet into the rushing stream. As it was, the unexpected shock drove him to his knees. Reaching back he caught an armful of leathery stuff and pulled, wincing as knife-like little teeth sliced through his hide.

He held a scarlet, wriggling horror in his hands.

Its body was furred, lean and sinewy, and as big as a small cat. From its shoulders sprang huge flimsy batlike wings. Snarling and spitting it struck at his hand, eyes of blazing fury, fanged jaws gaping wide. He did not need the sight of the long, curved, terrible canine fangs to know the scarlet horror for what it was—a *photh*, one of the monstrous blood-drinking vampire bats that infested the southernmost jungles.

Growling a curse, he broke its back with a twist of his great hands, and flung the vile thing from him.

But they were all around him now, a shrieking cloud of the great scarlet bats—for the photh hunt in packs, and therein lies the terror of them. In his days as a bandit chieftain in these same jungles, Thongor had seen a full-grown buck kroter go down under a flapping, obscene blanket of the scarlet horrors, who sucked the hapless beast bone-dry within minutes.

He sprang to his feet, brandishing the long pole. The raft was making swift progress and, could he survive the next few minutes, the headlong rush of the current might well carry him beyond the photh pack, and out of danger. But could he survive that long?

Muscles gliding under his bronzed hide, he brandished the heavy pole swiftly. Bat after scarlet bat he knocked from the air with a meaty thunk, breaking their spines or snapping the thin bones of their delicate wings. But a fluttering crowd of the vile things hung about his battling form, snapping at his face.

One landed on his bare thigh, needle-like claws piercing the skin as it clung. He tore it off—only to feel the fangs of another gnashing at his throat as a second came to cling at his shoulder. He ripped it loose, but a third now clung on his back, well between his shoulders where he could not easily reach it. Struggling amidst the snarling, snapping cloud of flapping horrors, he first lost his pole—and then his footing.

Cold rushing water closed over his head, gushing into his eyes and ears and his open mouth. He sank like a stone for an instant, then struck out with powerful arms. His head broke water; tossing back his wet mane from his face with a savage twist of his head, he peered about through the gathering gloom.

The raft was some yards away, being carried down the river more swiftly, now that it was relieved of his weight. Within moments it would be beyond his reach. But the scarlet vampire bats had fled him as he struck the water. That was a good thing to know—the photh did not like a ducking.

Sucking a deep breath into his lungs, Thongor sank under the waves and struck out for his rapidly disappearing raft. He swam with the sinuous twist and surging shoulders of a born swimmer—for all that he had learned the art first in his middle twenties. Ere long he reached his raft and powerful fingers closed on the rear of it. But still the squeaking cloud of flying horrors hovered about the raft . . . so Thongor wisely remained submerged until at length the vampires fell behind, weary of the fruitless pursuit. Then he hauled himself up on the raft again, and examined his injuries. The needle-sharp fangs of the vampire bats had slashed his flesh in a score of places, but the numbing venom of their fangs dulled what pain he might otherwise have felt. The wounds were neither deep nor serious; the cold clear waters of the Jungle River had washed them clean, and the photh's venom was not poisonous.

But the attack of the vampire bats had been a warning. The jungles were beautiful, but deadly. Like a gilded and gorgeous trap they were, and death waited for the unwary intruder lulled by the magnificence of the scenery. Thongor resolved to remain alert, his weapons close to hand. For the jungle was home to many other dangers beside the photh . . .

*

WHEN it became near to night again, and would soon be too dark to continue his passage down the river, he poled ashore, moored his raft in a secure place, and went hunting. This time he was lucky enough to kill a zulphar—no mean feat for one armed only with slender javelins whose tips were only fire-hardened wood instead of keen bladed steel. The zulphar, the wild boar of the Lemurian jungles, is a ferocious opponent, and very frequently its wild squealing charge and chomping jaws turn hunter into hunted. But the Barbarian took to the trees, found a path worn through the underbrush where generations of beasts had come to the margin of the river to drink, and waited—waited with that impassive and feline patience that was part of his savage heritage.

At length his vigil was rewarded. Green leaves parted and the ferocious devil-mask of a full-grown zulphar emerged from the undergrowth, snorting its warning to the jungle, pig-like little red eyes peering about suspiciously, bristled jaws open to reveal the terrible yellow tusks that could crush a man's thigh to jelly, pulverizing even the heavy bones.

Thongor could scarcely see through the dense gloom, for night was upon the jungle now. But his first javelin took the zulphar in the fatty part of the neck, just behind the ear. Only the coiled strength of Thongor's mighty thews could have hurled his flimsy missile with such force as to penetrate the thick flesh. As it was, his first javelin did not kill the beast, but severed its spinal cord, partially paralyzing the astounded and outraged boar.

Shrieking with rage and fury, foam slavering from the chomping jaws, the zulphar turned at bay. Even though its hind-quarters were but limp weight, dragging and useless, the fighting spirit of the savage brute was undimmed. Taking aim with enormous care, Thongor hurtled the second javelin—it struck with a meaty smack that was audible in the jungle hush—and the great boar fell dead, Thongor's javelin quivering deep in its heart.

An hour later, gorged on delicious boar steak, Thongor settled down in the crotch of a towering jannibar tree to spend his second night in the jungles of Ptartha. His sleep was deep and refreshing, and without dreams.

*

TOWARDS noon the next day, Thongor again found himself battling for his life.

He had, this time, hacked away a few choice flank steaks from the boar's carcass to relieve him of the tiresome chore of hunting his food afresh for every meal. Perhaps it was this, the tempting odor of fresh bloody meat, that drew the uncanny predator of the river to attack him. At any rate—without the slightest warning—his raft shuddered and side-slipped, and a great glistening head rose beside it, blunt-nosed and wedge-shaped, fanged jaws agape to freeze his blood with a terrible hissing cry.

A pampered, city-bred child of civilization might have found himself frozen, unable to act, petrified by the sudden and terrible appearance of the ghostly poa. But years of city-dwelling had not sapped or weakened Thongor's fighting instincts. He reacted with that hair-trigger speed centuries of life in the savage Northlands wilderness had bred deep in his ancestors, and which was stamped deep in Thongor, blood and brain and bone.

He held in his hands a long pole, wherewith he had been navigating his passage down the river. His first such pole had been lost the previous day when the scarlet, blood-drinking bats had attacked him. Then he had dropped the pole to fight—and fell into the waves of the Amadon himself, while the lost pole was whirled away in the rushing waters.

After eluding the horde of scarlet vampires, and before taking his rest that night, the Valkarthan had taken the precaution of cutting and trimming another such pole. This time he had selected a shaft of deep purple wood, heavy as teak, dense and strong—the young sapling of what would one day otherwise have grown into a towering jannibar tree, as the Lemurians called this species of Jurassic conifer. Thirteen feet long, two inches of solid wood thick, the great pole might have weighed as much as thirty pounds. Driven by the surging strength of his mighty thews, with all the steely strength of broad shoulders, deep chest, massive back and sinewy arms, the pole was a terrible and deadly weapon in the hands of one such as Thongor.

Now the long pole came whistling from the rushing waters to smack the hissing poa aside. The impact of Thongor's blow knocked the heavy head of the river dragon to one side with an audible *krakk* that sounded like a massive hammer smacked into cold meat. Powerful as the blow was, it did but daze the colossal reptile.

The raft lurched, as the poa lifted a portion of its long snaky length upon the surface of the rude raft. Muscles bunched along Thongor's broad shoulders as he swung the pole in a second terrific blow—but this time the poa snapped the pole out of his hands. Fangs sank in the tough wood and the shaft was wrenched from his grasp with a savage force that nearly sent him headlong into the water.

The mighty Valkarthan unsheathed his great broadsword and swung to the fray. The keen edge of the whistling steel bit deep in the ropy muscles of the poa's neck. Reeking black reptilian gore jetted forth to squirt its vileness across the warrior's naked thighs.

With a twist of his wrist, he tore the blade loose and swung it back—tracing an arc of gory droplets through the steamy air—for a second blow.

But the terrible snake-head thrust forth like an arrow, darting for his face—!

There was no help for it. A broadsword requires the use of both hands—and Thongor had no recourse but to let his sword fall while his hands flashed to seize and check the snake-head before its jaws closed upon his throat.

The steel blade of Sarkozan flashed in the sun as it fell in the rushing river and was lost.

With a terrific crash the raft fell apart under the threshing coils of the enraged poa. One glassy coil whipped in a shower of splattering foam to settle about his lean waist. The coil grew tight with crushing force. Locked in the grip of the poa, Thongor fell into the water amidst the wreckage of his raft and sank into the green depths, still battling.

Another massive coil ensnared his middle, and the lashing tail of the poa slid about his ankle. He had taken a mighty breath just before the flying spray and shattering foam had closed over his head. But he was in the watery domain of the poa now, and his chances of survival were greatly lessened.

The deadly coils constricted with mangling force, numbing his leg and all but pulping his waist. His lungs strained for air, his face blackened, his strength ebbed, but he fought on, using both hands to hold the serpent's head at bay.

Black blood poured from the great wound his sword had made in the reptile's glassy hide. It stained the dim water like a cloud of ink. Locked in combat, man and giant serpent settled to the muddy floor of the jungle river.

Thongor grimly knew he had but moments to live.

Releasing one hand, his other arm straightened, holding the wriggling neck and clashing jaws at arms' length, he whipped out the small needle-pointed dirk from its scabbard and drove it deep into the long wound he had made with his sword. Catching a firm grip, his blade buried in the serpent-flesh almost to the hilt, he *ripped* down with a burst of savage strength!

A billowing cloud of slimy black gore swirled up from the terrible wound. Despite its tremendous strength and mad fury, the poa felt the loss of blood and the searing agony of that great slashing cut. Its vitality ebbed. No longer did it struggle to crush the flailing limbs of the puny man-thing who had dared to challenge its watery domain—coils whipping away from Thongor's bruised and battered body, the poa sought only to escape.

But Thongor did not relax his iron grip on the serpent's throat. Still he ripped and sawed and tore at its vitals with that narrow dagger.

Then, with a terrific convulsion, the poa tore loose from his grip—and the dagger was left, deep-sunken in the serpent's coils. The wriggling lash of motion caused the reptile intense pain as the blade razored some internal organ. Mad fury drove all thought of escape from the terribly-wounded dragon, and again it hurtled itself at the warrior.

The recoil of the dragon's convulsion had thrust Thongor floundering some yards away across the width of the river's floor. His naked back scraped against the sharp edge of protruding rocks that thrust out of the mud and silt that carpeted the floor of the stream. Through eyes half-blinded by the roiling silt and gore, he dimly saw the glistening length of the savage poa as it flew again at his throat.

Thrusting out blindly with both hands to lever himself up from his prone position—his questing fingers found a familiar shape.

It was the hilt of Sarkozan, half buried in the mud!

With the last dregs of his strength he tore the sword loose and swung the glittering point to meet the rushing attack of the poa. The point flashed between the open jaws—sank deep in the tiny brain—and thrust out behind the base of the skull.

The poa, in its maddened rush, had impaled *itself* upon the broadsword's blade!

Leaving the reptile to lash through its death-throes, Thongor ripped his blade free and struck out for the surface. His lungs were nigh to bursting and his face was black with effort. With one final surge of fading strength, he dragged himself out of the stream and fell face down, exhausted, in the thick grasses.

The hilt of his Valkarthan broadsword was still clutched in his right hand.

*

NOW he must go forward on foot. For this portion of the jungle was made up entirely of huge and ancient trees, whose great roots had sapped the strength of their lesser competitors until only the hoary monarchs alone remained. Thongor's search found no saplings, nor even fallen branches of sufficient girth wherewith to construct a second raft. Henceforth, he must walk the way to the walls of the Pirate City.

It had not taken the mighty Barbarian very long to recover from the effects of his underwater struggle with the river dragon. The strength of his magnificent physique was very great, and his stamina—his iron endurance—was even greater. A lesser man, enervated and pampered by city life, would perchance have lain exhausted for days, rendered an invalid by such a toll on his strength. Not so with Thongor.

To live in the frozen and barren wilderness that had been his savage home is one constant and unceasing battle for survival. And in that battle only the hardiest may survive. Thus was he sprung from a line of mighty men—a hardy, pure-bred stock of warriors and hunters whose like no longer may be found in our modern world. Raised from the very cradle amidst the unending battle against hostile foes, savage beasts and the grim and wintry cold, every muscle of his mighty form had been trained to its fullest and most supple strength. Even his years of city life and kingship had not sapped his barbaric powers. His sheer animal vitality was such that an hour or two of rest sufficed to restore him to fighting trim again. A grim smile touched his impassive lips, as he cleansed the broadsword and slid it back in its worn leathern scabbard. 'Twas the luck of the gods had been with him there on the muddy floor of Amadon the Jungle River! Had he not found his lost sword—had he been forced to continue his jungle journey with empty hands—even such terrific strength and fighting courage as was his could not have protected him against the perils that lay ahead.

All that afternoon and night he plodded along beside the margin of the river. Tirelessly he cut a path through thick underbrush, never pausing for rest or food. Time was running out, and Tarakus—although by now it must be very near—lay he knew not how much farther ahead.

Indeed, it lay even nearer than he had dared to hope.

By dawn the jungle thinned and his sensitive ears caught the distant boom of mighty breakers crashing against wet black rock. Here the river curved away to the West to merge with the waters of the Gulf at last. He forded the river by means of overhanging boughs, for here the outstretched arms of the woodland monarchs intertwined above the rushing stream. Once across, he pressed on through the thinning foliage.

Suddenly he was at the edge of the jungle, and ahead, gaunt and black against the flame of morning, lay the rocky promontory at whose tip the Pirate City stood.

He loosened his blade from its scabbard and strode forth to look upon the city of his foemen.

And almost in the same instant, black against the flaming sky, the lithe figure of a fighting man with naked steel flashing in one hand, stepped forth to confront him—

CHAPTER 9:

SWORDS AGAINST PATANGA

The night is clear, the tide is fast,
Break out the sails once more!
We're forth upon the sea at last
To seek a golden shore . . .

—Sea Chantey of the Pirates of Tarakus

THE Inn of the Skull and Crossbones lay at the end of the Street of the Pawnbrokers, down near the less populated section of the waterfront. Here only vast warehouses and storage sheds rose; the houses, and by far the greater number of the other inns or wineshops, lay further up the slopes of the tiered city. It was for its very seclusion that Captain Redbeard and his men had chosen the Skull and Crossbones as their base. The Pirate City was filled with watchful eyes and listening ears; spies and enemies were everywhere, and there was hardly a man in all of Tarakus who would not betray a comrade for a bit of gold. Hence the crew of the *Scimitar* sought the most out-of-the-way lodgings they could find, for greater privacy.

Barim sat, this sundown, sprawled out in a great chair before a roaring fire, warming his weary legs and staring moodily into a leathern jack of ale. Across from him, in the open space between the tables and the long benches, the young Patangan warrior, Charn Thovis, prowled up and down, pacing restlessly as any caged beast might pace behind its hedge of iron bars.

Gusty wind whooped around the low eaves of the snug little inn. Cold sleety rain swept against the stout stone walls, rattling the huge oaken door and clattering against the mullioned panes of the little windows like skeleton fingers. Barim shivered, and drew his damp cloak closer about his burly shoulders. All day he had tramped the streets of Tarakus, seeking information. He had emptied his purse, buying drinks for garrulous seamen. He had talked himself hoarse bandying conversation with old comrades. And the sum total of what he had learned was disappointingly small.

This much they knew: Karm Karvus had indeed been held a prisoner by Kashtar the Red Wolf, Lord of Tarakus and king of the pirates. But Karm Karvus was missing. Many believed he had fallen to his death in the dark waters of that mighty subterranean cavern, for how could a man survive that fall into the cold black waves, where a mighty larth, goaded to madness by evil and age-old sorcery, roared and clamored for something to kill?

But whether or not the Prince of Tsargol had gone to a watery grave—or perchance had vanished into the gullet of a ravenous sea dragon—his whereabouts were as unknown as the fact of his death remained unproven. The merciless guards of Kashtar had scoured the streets and houses of the Pirate City from end to end, and they had found nothing. Nor could Belshathla, for all his vaunted powers of science and sorcery, discover the whereabouts of the missing captive with all his mastery of the occult arts. It was as if Karm Karvus had vanished from the surface of Lemuria . . .

Barim grunted at the mystery of it all, and, looking up, he met the pale, tense, and worried gaze of the young chanthar. The burly Redbeard dropped his eyes uncomfortably and a deep flush stained his bewhiskered cheeks. He knew what Charn Thovis was thinking, and although the young nobleman was too much the gentleman to ever give voice to his thoughts, Barim Redbeard could read them as plainly as if they were written on a page of parchment.

Or was it his own guilt he saw mirrored in the eyes of another? For deep within him, the bluff and hearty old rogue felt the gnawing pangs of self-accusation. Perhaps it was foolish of him to blame himself for the death of the Lord of the West . . . no man could have foreseen the chance that the *Scimitar* would be attacked by one of the great sea dragons of Yashengzeb Chun. No man could have dreamed of the wild accident of fate that had carried Thongor from the deck of the corsair galley into the trackless wastes of the Patangan Gulf, helpless in the grip of the gigantic sea monster. And no man could have done more than had Barim Redbeard to search for a sign of Thongor's survival.

For, delaying their passage to Tarakus, the men of the *Scimitar* had lingered long in those waters where Thongor had gone overboard, searching the waves with keen and hopeful eyes. And even after they had lifted anchor, instead of pressing on immediately for the harbor of the Corsair Kingdom, they had turned aside to shore, searching cove and bay and endless stretches of jungled shore, before at last giving up their quest and hoisting anchor for Tarakus.

As a matter of fact, young Charn Thovis did not in the least feel that old Redbeard was guilty of anything. Thongor had gone to his death as he had lived, facing peril with ready courage and shining steel. And, although the young warrior felt deeply the loss of his mighty king, he knew that no man had been responsible. And, in the shadow of the terrible danger that hung now, gathering like a storm, impending upon the destiny of Patanga and the Empire, even Charn Thovis was busied with more pressing worries than merely mourning a man he believed to be dead. Time enough to feel the loss of the great Barbarian when all these present dooms and dreads were past: for the moment, Patanga stood in deadly danger of imminent destruction, and Charn Thovis paced the inn restlessly, not so much from sorrow over the loss of Thongor, but from a haunting inward feeling of helplessness. For he could think of nothing that they could do to lift this doom from Patanga . . .

Part of their trouble stemmed from the unfortunate fact that they did not know exactly what would have been Thongor's plan of action. What had the Valkarthan intended to do upon reaching the Pirate City? Failing to find Karm Karvus, what would he have done about the impending invasion? And, lacking their mighty leader, what could *they* do in his place? Doubtless the intrepid warrior-king would have launched into some daring scheme whereby to bring the Red Wolf of Tarakus to his knees . . . perhaps, Thongor would have taken action to destroy the Niangan devil-weapons, thus rendering the Tarakan corsair navy ineffectual for any fleet action against the City of the Flame.

So it all came down to this: what, if anything, could they actually do that would help prevent the attack on Patanga?

*

BUSY with their moody thoughts, neither Charn Thovis nor Barim Redbeard heard the tramp of booted feet on the wet cobbles outside, nor heavy fingers fumbling at the latch.

Suddenly the great oaken door crashed open. The gusty wind caught it and slammed it back against the wall, with a loud crash that sent Barim Redbeard roaring to his feet, his naked blade flashing in the firelight.

He relaxed, seeing who stood in the door.

"Flay me, mate, you nearly had a yard of steel in your gizzard, sneaking up on us like that," he growled, shoving the blade back in its scabbard with a clang.

"Sorry, Cap'n," fat old Blay wheezed, stomping in and wringing the rainwater from the hem of his patched and worn old cloak. " 'Twas that devil-blasted wind, it was, fair snatched the door-handle from my hands, it did. Ah, gods! Is they a drop o' wine in the shop to warm the guts of a fat old man what has been trampin' the streets o' Tarakus from dawn to dark, till he has nigh wore down the leather of his soles?"

Snorting and whuffling, dripping wet, the jovial moon-faced old Kovian came slouching in, wet boots squelching noisily at every step. Heaving a lusty sigh, he sank back in a comfortable chair with a groan of relief, slowly pulled off his boots and lay back toasting his toes while young Charn Thovis brought him a cup of wine.

"Ah, thank ye, lad!" he beamed. Redbeard glowered impatiently while Blay tossed the wine down his gullet and set the cup down with a sigh, wiping his mouth with the back of one hand.

"Well?" the Redbeard rumbled. "Any word? Any news? You can't have been out there all day without learning something, blast your fat guts!"

"Gently, Cap'n, gently does it . . . ah, perhaps just a drop more of that wine, eh, lad? Good!"

Growling, Barim watched while the fat old Kovian rogue drank off a second cup. And when at length the empty goblet rang against the oaken table, he repeated his query in an even louder tone.

Blay settled back with a little smirk of satisfaction on his friendly features.

"Well, now, Cap'n," he began comfortably, "when I set out this morn'n' I thought first to drop around The Black Galleon at the other end o' the Street of the Sailmakers. See, when I were younger, I shipped once with a fellow name of Kurao, a Cadorna-man; we sailed under Cap'n Yarak the Hook—they called him th' Hook on account of he lost his right hand once in a boardin' party, and had a steel hook screwed into th' stump just as handy as you please—"

"Belay all this bilge, and get down to business, you fat Kovian bundle o' blubber!" Redbeard roared.

Blay shot him a hurt glance. "Aye, aye, Cap'n . . . now where was I when ye . . . oh, yes. Well! This fellow, Kurao, see, he's a-sailin' now aboard the *Zangabal Queen,* which be in port right now, or so I heerd tell yestereve . . . well, Kurao, as it turned out, heh heh, he was in *port* all right, but he warn't in no condition to recognize an old pal like me, on account of he had taken aboard a mite too much brandy the night before . . . aye, aye, Cap'n, I'm gettin' to it near about as fast as I can, but I got to work my way up to it, like . . ." Blay shut his eyes and pursed his lips thoughtfully. "Now, where was I?"

"This Kurao was dead drunk," Charn Thovis said gravely.

"Aye, that was it! Thank you, lad. Now, then. While I was in The Black Galleon, who should stroll in but me ol' comrade Thurgan the One-Eyed, him what fought shoulder to shoulder with me that time we cut our way into the temple on Iophis Isle in the Southern Sea, and made off with the pearl eyes of the heathen idol, aye, and half the natives howling at our heels . . . well, ol' One Eye has risen in the world a mite since we saw those grand times together. I happened to remember hearing from an ol' sweetheart of mine, what I run into day afore yesterday at the Anchor and Cutlass, that he is now very close friends to Duranga Thool himself, you know, the chief lieutenant to old Red Wolf! Well, sez I, here's the very chance I been lookin' for . . . all I got to do is feed enough strong wine into me old pal One Eye an' maybe I can squeeze the sailin' plans out o' him, if I be real sly like . . ."

He paused, smacking his lips thirstily, and glancing about at the wine bottle which stood behind Charn Thovis.

"Well? Get on with it, man—speak up, can't you?" Redbeard demanded irritably.

Blay cleared his throat noisily.

"Hakk-kaff! 'Scuse me, Cap'n . . . bit of a cold in me throat, I fear . . . tramping them windy streets all day, then gettin' caught in the downpour like this . . . but goin' on, wet boots an' all . . . ah, lad, could ye kindly pour ol' Blay another drop or two of that fine vintage there behind of you . . . just for medicinal purposes, you understand! Ah . . . that's fine . . . well, then, just a bit more to finish off the bottle . . ."

He quaffed the red wine down thirstily while Redbeard sat, growling inarticulately and chewing on the inside of his cheeks. At length the fat man came up for air, blowing like a porpoise, wiping his mouth with the back of his hand.

"Ah, that feels better . . . now, just you let me see . . . where was—oh, yes! The sailin' plans, old One Eye, get him drunk. That was the scheme . . ."

Captain Barim snorted loudly. "Yes, and a sillier scheme I have not heard till now. Why, any fool could see through you as through a just-cleaned windy-pane. So what happened?"

"Ahem. I got the plan."

Silence reigned for a moment. Barim Redbeard and Charn Thovis exchanged an incredulous stare.

"You . . .?"

Blay beamed and chuckled, his full girth jiggling, bristling dirks twinkling to the seismic waves of inward laughter.

"Aye, Cap'n, worked like a charm, it did! Ol' One Eye, well, he never had much of a head for wine, although he doesn't dare admit it and swears he can drink half o' Tarakus-city under the table. So I matched him drink fer drink, while we swapped old times together, an' in no time I cracked him open like any egg, and he spilled his guts all over the floor, he did, danged if'n he didn't . . ." Blay shook his huge red jowls, beaming and chuckling at the thought.

"Blay, are you certain this Thurgan isn't smarter than you give him credit for being, and didn't know you were trying to get information out of him?" Charn Thovis asked anxiously.

Blay wheezed good-humoredly, laid a fat red finger beside his bulbous nose, and winked portentiously.

"Not him, me lad! Nay, old Blay was cunning about it . . . got to talking about all the jolly swag we'd stowed belowdecks in our time, and makin' guesses about the size of our share, when it came to dividin' up the loot of Patangy, and the first thing *I* know, he's daring me to guess when we sail . . . well, he was burstin' with the news, so I just sat back and let him pour it out . . ."

"Well, WHEN IS IT, you lubber?" Redbeard roared.

"Termorrow dawn," wheezed Blay.

"*Tomorrow?* But—it can't be!"

"Oh, aye, Cap'n! Look ye, the way One Eye Thurgan puts it: ol' Red Wolf has thrown over his plans o' carryin' off half the Sarks of the West, 'cause he's afeered Karm Karvus has escaped alive and is going t' bring the word to the Black Hawk, y'see . . . so the *old* plan is junked, an' the *new* plan is t' strike fast as lightnin' before Patangy can get word and spring t' arms, so termorrow dawn we sail . . . shippin' orders will be brought to each Cap'n of th' Coast tonight at midnight by messenger—"

Swearing lustily and dragging on his greatcoat, Barim

was on his feet roaring orders up the stairs to those of his weary and footsore crew as had already turned in.

"Durgan! Roegir, blast yer indigo hide! Zend . . . Thangmar, all you lubbers—look alive, there, for the love o' heaven!"

Lean, leathery old Durgan, his dour face stamped with bewilderment, peered over the rail at the roaring captain below.

"Wh-what's the alarm, Cap'n!" he quavered.

"The alarm is we sail in thirty minutes, so stir your bones, you one-eyed rogue! With dawn the fleet of Tarakus sails for a surprise attack on Patanga, and we had best be undersail to bring them the word . . . pray to Gorm and Shastadian we reach the City o' Fire in time!"

*

THEY went roaring and blustering out into the sleety cold, stamping and blowing and cursing lustily, the men grumbling at being torn, in some cases bodily, out of their snug warm beds, but Barim Redbeard was afire with eagerness to be gone. No time to rouse the slumbering landlord and fetch the kroters from the stable. Nothing would satisfy the Redbeard but they go running down the Street of the Pawnbrokers in full tilt, the door of the Skull and Crossbones swinging open and unlatched at their heels.

Down to the docks they piled, slipping on the wet cobbles, shivering against the cold wet blasts of wind, while a crazy moon peered and leered at them with one mad eye glaring down through scudding wisps of flying cloud.

Down the long stone quay they ran, Redbeard, swearing lustily, in the lead, his kerchief snapping in the wind, sea-spume on his fiery bush of whiskers, his great sea boots slapping the wet stone dock ringingly. Ahead the black hull of the *Scimitar* rode the choppy waters, sails furled and mooring lamps burning red and green and yellow.

"Ahoy, the *Scimitar!*" the Redbeard bellowed. "Look alive on deck, you lubbers! Down with the ladder, mates, we sail now!"

An astonished Zangabali, nightshirt flapping about his skinny shanks, peered down at them from the deck-rail.

"That you, Cap'n?"

"Of course it's me, you lazy rogue, over the side with that rope ladder and rouse those slumbering dogs—we sail for Patanga on the instant! *Move,* you lubber, or I'll scuttle ye and spread ye out for fish-bait—"

"B-but, Cap'n, we *can't* sail," the Zangabali quavered.

"And why not, tell me that? When Barim Redbeard says sail, then sail we do!"

Leaning over the rail, the half-clad seaman pointed one bare arm.

"The tower! Look at the signal-lamps! They closed the Sea Gate at sunset, Cap'n, we can't get out o' the harbor now!"

Redbeard stifled a growled curse and turned, craning his neck, to blink up at the tall stone tower that lifted from the very end of the long rocky promontory, where white billows thundered in sheets of flying spray against black fangs of naked rock. Blue and yellow the signal lamps shone through the moonlit night . . . blue and yellow . . . and that meant the impregnable Sea Gates were closed for the night, and no ship could sail forth from the walled harbor of Tarakus.

"Now, by the Eleven Scarlet Hells," the Captain swore softly. Charn Thovis looked at him in puzzlement. "Barim—what is it? What do those lamps mean? Why can't we set sail?"

The Captain sighed heavily. "The harbor is enclosed in a great circle," he groaned. "Half o' this circle is the curve of the city waterfront . . . the rest o' the harbor is sheltered by those stone breakwaters you see there, and there. There be only one open channel through which ships can make passage, and that cunning red dog, Kashtar, has built his Sea Gates there . . ."

"What are these Sea Gates, then?" Charn Thovis persisted.

"Great chains, lad, chains of massive bronze, with links that weigh half a ton each . . . four great chains across the mouth of the open way, locked to mighty rings bolted deep in the stone o' the breakwater. When the chains are locked in place, the Sea Gates are closed, as they say . . . and 'twould take half an army to open them, for Kashtar has builded him twin citadels of stone one to either end of the breakwater, with a permanent garrison of a hundred or so warriors there, to guard the Sea Gates . . . far too many for a small crew such as we to fight our way through, even if we could somehow unlock the great chains . . . no, lad, I fear that crafty dog, Kashtar, has outsmarted us. Doubtless he thought there might be a spy or two among the Captains o' the Coast, and in case any were willin' to betray his plans to Patanga for red gold, he had the Sea Gates closed with sundown, so that not a single ship could sail . . . all right, mates, back to the Skull 'n' Crossbones!"

Charn Thovis swore feelingly, but there was nothing else to do. The weight of cold reason was on the side of Barim Redbeard.

Old Blay peered out to sea, and snuffled a little, wiping his nose with one red hand.

"Them poor folks back in Patangy," he muttered soberly. "Sound asleep in they beds, trustin' to the good men o' the *Scimitar* to bring 'em warning in time, and to the Black Hawk, bless 'im, to foil the plot somehow . . . and now the first thing they'll know of the invasion is when they wake up termorrow mornin' an find the black ships of Tarakus in they harbor and the grinnin' rogues of Tarakus battlin' through they streets . . . ah, me!"

Sighing gustily, the friendly old Kovian shook his head despairingly. One by one the men straggled back through the cold wet streets, to the inn and to their beds. And they found at the door of the Skull and Crossbones an officer of Kashtar Red Wolf bearing shipping orders. With dawn the *Scimitar* was to set sail in the last rank of the fleet and sail against Patanga.

What chance had the City of the Flame, all unsuspecting that the assault was to be launched in mere hours? When the swords of the Corsair Kingdom went up against Patanga, what chance for freedom to survive in the World's West?

BOOK THREE

AGAINST THE STORM

"For this was the sin of the Gray Magicians of Nianga, that they in their folly and lust for power had transgressed the commandments of the Nineteen Gods . . . they had ventured beyond the limitations the Gods had set on the inquiries of man's quest for knowledge and wisdom, and the hellish weapons their dark studies had created were as a stench and as an abomination in the nostrils of Heaven . . . wherefore were they smitten with the Divine Wrath and all their works were set at naught . . ."

—*The Great Book of Sharajsha the Wizard*

CHAPTER 10:

YIAN OF CADORNA

Thus with the aid of Father Gorm,
There in the stronghold of the foe,
He found a shelter from the storm
While soldiers searched for him below . . .

—The Tsargol Records

THE slim figure, veiled in clinging silks, struggled under in his grasp. Suddenly, Karm Karvus stifled a gasp of astonishment. For his hands had encountered—not the hard muscles of a man—but the yielding softness of a woman! He snatched his hands away and stepped back.

"Do you always enter a lady's chamber in so rude a manner, Prince of Tsargol?" the woman, or rather, the girl, demanded coolly. Rearranging her garments, she turned a face of astonishing beauty upon him. To his amazement, Karm Karvus saw that this was no painted and bedizened wineshop slut, no pirate chieftain's wanton, but a young woman of birth and breeding and dignity.

"Your pardon, my lady, I did not realize . . . but how is it that you know me?"

She regarded him coolly; then, relenting a little, she smiled. "When half the city is being turned inside out to find a fugitive named Karm Karvus, it requires no special intelligence to assume that you are the man," she said in a soft, husky voice. "Who else but a fugitive from Kashtar's prisons would be clambering over the rooftops on such a foul night? But come, you have naught to fear from me—I, too, am a prisoner of the Red Wolf, Yian of Cadorna is my name. You are weary, cold, wet from the storm. Here is wine and meat, and a roaring fire. And I believe I can find you some dry garments—"

Fumbling for some awkward words of gratitude, he relaxed in a chair by the fire, removing his rain-soaked boots and feeling the crackling warmth bake the fatigue and chill from his bones. As the girl, Yian of Cadorna, busied herself in tending to his needs, his gaze followed her curiously.

She was young, surely no more than twenty, and slim and regal, with the clear golden skin of Cadorna, oblique dark eyes, almond-shaped, slightly tilted, sparkling like black jewels. Her hair was a torrent of heavy black silk that poured down her slim shoulders to her waist. She had a soft warm mouth, ripe for kissing, and beneath a complicated garment of thin clinging silken stuff, her body was lithe and supple and deliciously rounded.

Cadorna, he knew, was westernmost of the Nine Cities. It lay beyond Kovia, up the outer curve of the continent, on the shores of the Southern Sea. The cities of the Gulf had little commerce with far Cadorna, but this was due to its seclusion and remoteness, not to policy. For the Lord of Cadorna, Prince Kazan, was not unfriendly and had exchanged embassies with the court of Thongor. Now that he thought of it, Karm Karvus recalled that he had heard Prince Kazan had a young daughter . . . but what was she doing here, in the stronghold of the pirates of Tarakus?

She must have read the question in his eyes, or perchance it was her woman's gift of intuition. For when he thanked her for the strong red wine and the spiced meats she set before him, she explained her presence in the city.

"I, too, was taken captive by the corsairs and am being held as a hostage against my father's complicity with the demands of the sea wolves," she said. In swift words she described how she had been sailing in her pleasure boat down the coast from Cadorna when her vessel had been attacked by the pirates. Her courtiers and attendants had all been slain resisting the boarding party and she herself had been carried back to Tarakus a prisoner. Karm Karvus listened in grim silence: it would seem that the plans of Kashtar were to seize a hostage from every royal house of the West and use their persons to gain entry into each of the Nine Cities. He asked her if she knew of other such royal captives, but the girl shook her head, the great bell of her shimmering black hair swinging entrancingly about her heart-shaped, elfin face.

"Besides you and I, Kashtar has taken no other captives," she said gravely. Then she smiled, her face lightening. "The Pirate King is having his difficulties with me," she laughed. "I, too, tasted the rather rude hospitality of his foul and stinking dungeons for a time, but when Kashtar saw that the hardships I endured were only making my refusals to assist his schemes even more obdurate, he cunningly immured me here, in relative comfort, with ladies to attend to my wants. He hoped to soften me with a touch of luxury; later to threaten to return me to the dungeon cell if I continued to resist. But thus far I have held out."

"Surely you are not left alone and unguarded?"

She shook her head. "Indeed, no. While I have the privacy of these upper chambers to myself, guards are stationed on the ground floor and it is impossible for me to leave the building. For they assume that a softly-reared Princess could never go climbing about the rooftops of the city, as you have been doing. However, as a matter of fact, I have been contemplating just that mode of escape, and was at the window just now, examining the terrain with just that in mind—when I saw you climbing towards my chamber. I lit the lamp so that I could catch your attention. I had intended to let you in—but I had not expected you would come crashing through the panes uninvited!"

The Tsargolian flushed. "Princess, I—"

She laughed softly. "No need to apologize . . . a desperate man seeks any haven in the storm. But here, for a time at least, you are quite safe. The soldiers have already searched this building hours ago. But, come, what are your plans?"

Karm Karvus frowned. He had been kept so busy merely eluding recapture that he had not had much leisure wherein to formulate any practical plan of escape from the city. Rather awkwardly, he was forced to admit as much. And here, it seemed, the girl was far ahead of him. For she had been busy during the long days of her captivity. From a low chest she removed sheets of heavy parchment and spread them out for his perusal.

"From this window I have enjoyed a good view of the city, and this crude map shows the layout of the streets rather well," she pointed out. "Like you, I had planned to escape over the rooftops, for that avenue seems to entail the slightest risk of discovery. I had hoped for a dark and moonless night for my attempt at escape. Here is the city wall, along the northern side of the promontory . . . there are the gates. They seem to be not only very heavily guarded, but well lighted as well. However, my observations have shown that no guards patrol the top of the wall . . . hence if we can gain this sector of the wall undiscovered—"

"We? Surely, Princess, you do not think I can gamble your safety as well as my own!" Karm Karvus protested.

She regarded him with a calm, level glance.

"If I do not go in your company," she said firmly, "then I shall go alone. Now, then, notice the roof of this building here . . . it thrusts out much further than the others . . . with a bit of luck, and some agility, we can leap from the edge of this roof to the top of the wall. I have already woven several lengths of cloth together into a sort of ladder, using thick knots in the fabric in place of rungs. We can tie one end of this length of cloth around the merlon of any one of these crenelations and thus lower ourselves down outside the walls . . ."

Karm Karvus rather feebly tried to argue the dangers of such an expedition, the hazards of discovery, the perils of slippery tiles, and the difficulties of clambering over wave-lashed rocks to the base of the promontory, and thence into the thousand deadly dangers of the jungles through which they must find passage before reaching the nearest friendly city. But Yian of Cadorna turned a deaf ear to his protestations.

"Listen to me, Prince of Tsargol," she said firmly. "I am no pampered and delicate maiden, I assure you. I can ride as well as a man, and hunt. I am practiced with the sword and the bow and can hold my own in combat with any man. My beloved father has often bemoaned his lack of strong sons, so in so far as I have been able I have trained myself to take a son's place in his affections. In this matter I will listen to no arguments, for I am going, either with you or without you."

"But, Princess—!"

"—Kashtar of Tarakus thinks to use me as a key to unlock the gates of my father's city. But I refuse to be the instrument of the downfall of my house. If the doom of our dynasty comes, if the freedom of Cadorna the Golden is lost before the force of some oppressor, it shall not come through me, for far rather would I go down to the cold halls of the restless dead, than be the tool of the destruction of my people. This I have sworn to the Gods of my city, and in this matter I will brook no opposition!"

Karm Karvus made some further objections, but gradually they subsided. The Prince of Tsargol was not the first man to lose an argument with a woman, nor was he the first to discover the futility of pleading reason and common sense with a woman who has already made up her mind. So, in the end, he resolved to take her with him.

*

THE storm at last blew over, and they were ready to depart. Yian disappeared for a moment, then reappeared in new raiment. Pointing out that thin silks were hardly fitted to clambering over rooftops, she had changed into tight-fitting breeches of supple suede that showed off her long and slender legs to their best advantage. She had also donned knee-high boots of light, flexible leather, a long-sleeved blouse, and a warm woolen cloak against the cold. Her long black hair was braided back so that it would not encumber her arms, and a kerchief was tied about her brows. With her bright, sparkling eyes and the fresh color in her cheeks, and her long limber form, she looked like a beautiful boy in the tight breeches and swashbuckling cloak.

For the Prince, she had supple doeskin buskins to replace his water-soaked boots whose leather had cracked and split. Fresh dry clothing and a warm cloak such as her own completed his costume. These garments she had found in an old chest in an unused room.

The rain had stopped, but the Moon was still hidden behind thick-piled stormclouds, so they might be able to make their escape unobserved, with luck.

They set forth without delay, Yian having committed to memory the landmarks of her rude chart of the streets. Cursing himself for a fool, Karm Karvus helped the Princess over the sill. Why had he permitted himself to be burdened with her presence—surely the girl would not be able to climb the roofs as ably as himself. After all, he was a trained and limber warrior, in the full prime of his muscular manhood—

Of course, almost the first thing that happened, was that Karm Karvus lost his footing on the slippery tiles, and fell about a dozen feet down the rain-wet tiles of the steep-sided roof, until he managed to break his fall by seizing a chimney. Dangling awkwardly by one hand, it did no good to his self-esteem to watch the Princess come nimbly down the sloping roof to his rescue, as sure-footed as any mountain goat. He was surprised at the steely strength of the girl as she hauled him to his feet again and assisted him back to the peak of the roof. And thereafter he made no further complaints as to the complications her presence afforded.

From roof to roof they went, at times swinging across the narrow cobbled alleys, and at times being forced to leap from the edge of one roof to the edge of another. Without any further accidents they came, at length, to the edge of the city and looked down upon the wall that guarded this side of Tarakus from attack.

Yian of Cadorna had laid her plans well. This portion of the wall was dark and unguarded, lying as it did midway between two gates. It should not have been very difficult to leap from the roof ledge to the top of the city wall, for the wall was broad enough for two guards to walk abreast and the other edge of the wall was crenelated so that one could not very easily over-estimate the leap and fall off.

Except, of course, that Karm Karvus slipped again.

His boot-heels slid in a puddle of rainwater just as he was gathering his strength for the hazardous leap into space. The result was that he went skidding and sliding to the brink of the roof and toppled over, hurtling down to the rain-wet cobbles below.

He might well have broken his leg or even his neck, but as luck would have it, one of the guardians of the gate was patrolling the inner wall on kroter-back, and this unfortunate was passing directly beneath him as Karm Karvus fell.

He landed full on the shoulders of the astounded guard, and the two of them went tumbling from the saddle, as the kroter squealed and bucked in its fright.

Karm Karvus was on his feet in a moment, and before the half-stunned guard could marshal his groggy wits, the Prince of Tsargol knocked him unconscious with a well-placed right to the jaw. Out cold, the guard went sprawling backwards into the inky shadows.

Karm Karvus peered about swiftly, but it seemed the guard had been alone and that the brief flurry of activity had aroused the attentions of no one. Silently he cursed his luck, but then he paused to reason that at least the accident had gained him a weapon. For he unbuckled with swift hands the baldric of the guard and settled the embossed leather about his own shoulder. Now he had a sword, and he was delighted to see that it was a slim rapier of Tsargolian make, the very weapon with which he was most familiar. Swiftly he disarmed the guard, taking a long-bladed dagger from his harness. Then he bound and gagged the unconscious guard in strips of tough cloth torn from the guard's own cloak, and rolled the body well back into the shadows where chances of his discovery were slight. As for the kroter, he tethered the beast to a drainpipe nearby, securely tying him with his own reins so that he should not return with an empty saddle to the guard-house and thus cause suspicion and alarm.

Yian had been anxiously watching all this from the roof-ledge overhead. Now she took the only step possible. Their fortunes were in hazard now that they were seperated, and they must rejoin each other at the first opportunity.

Measuring the distance between the edge of the roof and the top of the wall with her eye, the girl gathered all her strength. Keeping a cool head, she bent double—and launched herself into space with a mighty leap—

Watching from below, Karm Karvus felt his heart rise into his mouth as he saw that slim figure flying through space. How easy it would be for her to miss, to slip, to loose her footing! One miscalculation, and she would hurtle to the slick cobbles below.

But Yian of Cadorna had not lied when she said that she had trained her body like a man. She landed nimbly atop the wall with inches to spare—and was safe. Now she swiftly unwound the knotted length of cloth from about her shoulders and let one end fall down the inner side of the wall to within reach of Karm Karvus's hand.

Swiftly and silently, the young warrior Prince climbed the length of knotted cloth hand over hand, and within moments he rejoined her—drawing himself up over the edge of the wall. The outer edge of this wall was deeply crenelated with rising merlons and gaping crenels like a sawtooth blade. The Princess had swiftly tied a noose around the base of one merlon, and therefrom had let the crude ladder dangle down the inner side of the wall. Now that Karm Karvus had gained the top of the wall and stood beside her, she drew the knotted ladder up and flung it down the outer wall. Using the thick knots for handholds, Karm Karvus and the girl swiftly descended to the jumbled mass of wet black rocks below. Spray exploded in blinding sheets of white spray about them, the tumbled and broken rocks were slimy with moss and mold underfoot—but they were over the wall and on their way to freedom at last!

As swiftly as possible, they clambered over the great slippery masses of jumbled rock. There was hardly any chance of an alert eye observing them as they traveled the length of the promontory, for in the confusion of black stone and thundering spray they were hardly likely to be visible from above. But should the Moon emerge from behind her mantle of stormy clouds, the danger of chance discovery would be greatly increased.

Thus, taking care not to miss their footing, but making all possible speed, Karm Karvus and Yian of Cadorna clambered swiftly and silently over the broken rocks towards the mainland of the continent, where relative safety lay in the edges of the jungles of Ptartha.

*

WET, bedraggled, and weary, with aching arms and tired legs, they at last gained the base of the promontory. As yet, it seemed, no one had discovered either Yian's absence or the means whereby they had made their escape over the walls of the Pirate City.

It was shortly before dawn. Already the skies of the East were dim with pale and ghostly flame, and the stars burned less fiercely through rents in the cloud-veiled skies. Day would be here soon.

Before them the jungle rose like a wall of black emerald. It was mysterious and gloomy, its impassive silence broken only by vagrant whispers and the rustling of small creatures padding through the matted underbrush.

Now they had left their human enemies behind; but new and more terrible foes lay deep within the hush of the jungle gloom—the savage predators whose hunting grounds they were about to enter. Their human foes they had eluded with cleverness and cunning, but Karm Karvus knew that only strength and courage and shining steel could defend them against the dripping jaws of the denizens of the Ptarthan jungles.

Gesturing to the girl to keep well behind him, he advanced to the margin of the jungle, drawing his sword. No sooner had he but taken the first few steps into the emerald gloom, however, than a black and towering shape loomed up directly in his path. It had materialized out of nowhere with the speed and silence of some grim phantom.

Without a moment's hesitation, Karm Karvus lunged. The naked blade in his fist sped glittering as he thrust at the heart of their unknown adversary—

CHAPTER 11:

THE ARMADA OF DOOM

More strong than talisman or rune
Or visions conjured from the moon,
Or arts of sorcerer or seer
Is one strong man who knows not fear.

—The Scarlet Edda

DAWN rose over the edges of the world, lighting all the skies with a brilliance of gold and crimson flame.

Ere the first light glowed in the East, the hosts of Tarakus were awake. Hundreds of grinning corsairs, armed to the teeth, poured down the long stone quays and filed aboard the slim galleys with the long black hulls.

There were spearmen and bowmen, swordsmen and sling-throwers, men to man the catapults and the fire-arrows. Warriors from all the cities of the South were there, dark-eyed and black-haired Turanians from Shembis and Tsargol, Thurdis and Zangabal . . . swarthy-hued desert warriors from Vosashpa with purple-dyed beards and lean, hard-faced warriors from Darundabar and Dalakh below the Mountains of Ardath . . . towering giants from the Red Forests of Kodanga country were there as well, with their long blond hair woven in thick braids, and a few of the mighty Blue Nomads, renegades fled from the justice of the hordes that roamed and ruled the Great Plains of the East . . . yellow-skinned, almond-eyed Cadornyana, and slender sallow-faced men from Pelorm and Tarakus itself, with silky black moustaches and vicious, cold eyes.

And in the heart of every man that poured aboard the waiting corsair fleet burned the lust for gold and gems, for wine and women. Soon, they knew, and grinned hungrily at the knowledge, the fabulous wealth of rich and glorious Patanga would be theirs. When the heavy treasure chests of the City of the Flame opened to pour a glittering flood of golden riches at their feet, not a corsair of their number but would be wealthy for life, a landed lord, with gold enough to live his years in luxury and splendor. They laughed at the thought, and fingered the gemmy hilt of dirk and dagger and keen-bladed cutlass . . . soon the sea wolves would run amok through the broad avenues of mighty Patanga, and the golden wealth of Earth's most glorious Empire would flow at their feet . . .

Long ere dawn rose above the borders of the world, Belshathla was awake and at work. The Gray Magician checked and rechecked the weird instrument of twinkling brass rods and mysterious crystal globes bolted to the foredeck in the flagship of Kashtar himself. All was well, and no harm had come to the Lamp of Madness, doubly precious now that it alone survived the destruction that the cunning of Karm Karvus, or perhaps the vainglorious pride and vanity of the Gray Magician himself, had wreaked on its only duplicate.

An unholy lust burned in the cold eyes of Belshathla as he envisioned the horrors that the Gray Death would bring down upon Patanga, as his hand—*his* hand!—swept the towering battlements of the City of the Flame with madness, murder and death!

Now came Kashtar himself, surrounded with his chief lieutenants, hanging on his word for last instructions. His slim figure resplendent in scarlet, the Pirate King of Tarakus surveyed the might of his great armada as it rode to anchor under the first faint light of dawn there in the vast enclosed harbor of the Pirate City. No greater naval expedition had ever been launched in all the long and crimson annals of warfare . . . and almost within his grasp, it seemed, lay the summit of his ambitions, the Throne of the World itself. Cold fires blazed up in his somber eyes as he envisioned the mighty Thongor in chains, forced to kneel before the Flame Throne, at the feet of Kashtar the Red Wolf! What a glorious moment of triumph that would be, and how he longed to see it dawn . . .

"All is in readiness, Wolf," his chief lieutenant, a swarthy and bewhiskered rogue named Duranga Thool, reported. Kashtar nodded somberly. For a moment he gazed about him, exulting in the heights of his power, his lungs drinking in the fresh salt tang borne to his nostrils on the keen winds of dawn. Then he gave the word.

"Open the Sea Gates!"

The word was passed from man to man to a sailor perched high in the rigging. This man lifted signal flags and gave the word to the twin citadels that guarded with unsleeping vigilance the mouth of the enclosed harbor.

But tiny mites at this distance, guards on the long seawall before the twin citadels bent their backs. Windlasses creaked, ropes drew taut, dawnfire flashed from water drops as the mighty brass links of the gigantic chain were hauled dripping from the depth. The chains parted and, at last, the channel lay free and open, with the empty waters of the Patangan Gulf beyond them.

Kashtar mounted to his own quarterdeck and gave the signal and the morning stillness was broken by the slow throb of drums as chanting seamen bent to the oars. The first rank of vessels began to draw up their sea anchors and turn in precision formation to leave the harbor.

Oars dipped to roil the waters, then rose flashing in the early light. Rose and fell and rose again. Like gigantic water insects, moving on slow spidery legs, the advance ships moved between the twin citadels into the open Gulf.

Rank by rank the ships began to move, and gradually, rising above the creak of the oarlocks, the boom of the drums, the wash and gurgle of the waves, came the full-throated song of the pirates of Tarakus, roared from half a thousand lusty throats . . .

The night is clear, the tide is fast,
Break out the sails once more!
We're forth upon the sea at last
To seek a golden shore . . .

Strong and fierce the corsair hymn rose on the clear fresh air of morning, growing ever greater in its strength, as the crew of ship after ship caught the tune and carried it echoing across the gliding waters . . .

The stars are bright, the wind is cold,
The moon is drifting free.
We're out to seek for pirate gold
Across a silver sea . . .

*

BUT one ship there was in all that vast armada that did not sing. Its lean black hull cutting the waves, brass-beaked dragon prow catching fire from the red light of dawn, scarlet sails spread and booming in the brisk wind, the *Scimitar* rode with the rear of the corsair fleet to the sack of the City of the Flame.

Pacing his quarterdeck, a moody scowl upon his frowning brows, Captain Barim Redbeard cudgeled his wits for some way out of this dilemma.

Beside him, pale and tense in the dawn, young Charn Thovis watched with a sinking heart as rank on rank of the pirate fleet, galleys and carracks and ships of war, sailed through the stone gates of the harbor on flashing oars, lifted full canvas, and turned sharp prows towards distant Patanga.

For the men of the *Scimitar* had no choice but to sail with their erstwhile brethren to the looting of Patanga, for all that their secret sympathies lay with Thongor's unsuspecting and beleaguered city. It was sail with the rest, or be suspected of black treason and hang from the yardarm.

Fat, friendly Blay and lean, dour, one-eyed old Durgan stood at the rail watching the red roofs of Tarakus fall away astern. The moon-faced old Kovian, no longer jovial, heaved a hearty sigh. And he exchanged a gloomy look with his lank and leathery comrade.

"How can we do it, mate?" Blay wheezed dispiritedly. "How can we hack and murther like the rest o' these wolves, in the rapine of a city of our friends? What will the little lad say when his old comrades come a-knockin' at the gates o' his father's royal city, with naked cutlasses in they hands, eh? O, 'twas a dark day for poor ol' Blay when he decided to turn pirate and seek his fortune on the high seas, that it were!"

Durgan grunted, and spat over the side.

"Never you mind, mate," he said. And, cocking his one good eye towards the tall and stalwart figure that stood black against the dawn-lit sky on the quarterdeck, he added in a low conspiratorial whisper: "As for me, I puts my trust in the Cap'n yonder! He's a deep one, he is . . . if any manjack of the lot o' us can figger a clear channel through these here troubled waters, why, it be him, and no other. You lay your confidence with 'im, 'cause I'll wager my share he's got a plan. A deep one, the Cap'n, aye . . . and a good one for plans, he is!"

"Aye, well . . . by Shastadian's green beard, comrade, I hope yer right," Blay groaned. "I do hope you be right . . ."

*

SLOWLY the towering heights of Tarakus fell away astern. A dark and hulking mountain of black shadow was Tarakus, looming up against the gold and crimson tapestries of dawn. White morning mist mantled the surface of the dark mirror that was its harbor. Above, moment by moment, the sky brightened. Pure golden flame spread blindingly, and now the topmost towers of the shadow-drowned city flamed with rose and lavender and palest gold as they caught the level shafts of light.

By now the last ships had left the harbor and rode under full sail upon the open waters of the Gulf. Far above, sunflame caught and edged with purest gold the crisp, curled clouds. The shadow-thronged dome of the sky lightened gradually to pale and luminous azure. And it was day.

At the quarterdeck rail, glowering out on the dancing waves, his great fiery red-gold bush of beard blowing in the brisk wind, Captain Barim pondered what he could do to shield helpless Patanga from the raging sea wolves of the Pirate City.

His chief officer, a small, dark-faced seaman named Angar Zend, his scarred face half-hidden behind thick bushy black whiskers, a gaudy red kerchief wound about his brows, came over to where the Captain stood.

"Well?" Angar Zend demanded. "What's the plan? Love o' Heaven, Cap'n, are ye going t' let us just sail right into Patanga harbor and put all them folk to the sword? Surely, ye have worked out some plan, sly dog that ye be. Let's hear it—out with it, Cap'n, by the Scarlet Hells!"

"Belay that bluff and swagger, Zend, ye black dog," the Captain roared. "Bluster at the men below, but I'll not have such temper on my quarterdeck—"

Charn Thovis came over to where they stood arguing.

"Yes, but Captain—what *is* your plan?" he asked.

Barim Redbeard narrowed his fierce blue eyes, squinting against the sun-glare.

"Well, men, here it is. We can't outrace Kashtar's whole armada and reach Patanga in time to give warning—not when we are sailing *with* the bloody armada, least-wise! And we can't fall back and lose them through a ruse, then somehow out-distance them to get there first. D'ye follow me, lads?"

"Aye, we're right on course with ye, Cap'n; so?" little Angar Zend growled.

"Very well, then. Now, Patanga has at least a fighting chance, look you, for her flying patrols are bound to spot the vanguard of the fleet long ere it heaves into port. Those flying airboats, armed with them lightning guns that clever sage, Iothondus, contrived some years agone, give them a powerful advantage, even against so mighty a fighting fleet as this, see?"

Charn Thovis and the first mate nodded.

"So, the way I sees it, the one thing that gives Kashtar an edge against the might o' Patanga is that cursed and devilish weapon bolted there on the foredeck of the Red Wolf—that Ray of Madness. Belshathla thinks to sweep the aerial navy from the skies with it, to sweep the harbor clean o' men, to drive mad whatever force comes up against the sea wolves . . . but if we can disable that hellish contraption and wreck the filthy thing, Patanga has a fighting chance to survive this whole fleet, aye, a damned good chance, sink me if it be not so!"

Angar Zend chewed on a tuft of bristling black whiskers, eyeing his captain sourly.

"Aye, all well and good, Cap'n, but how in blazes do ye expect to get at the raygun on the flagship, an us here in the very last rank o' the corsair fleet?" he growled.

The Redbeard winked conspiratorially, and laid one finger beside his nose. "Ah! As fer that, Zend, the fleet will be a-sailin' all day, and p'raps all night as well. But there be mighty fogs on the great Gulf in this cold month, drawing towards winter, and mayhap—in the darkness o' night, thick with fog—we can detach ourselves from the main body o' the fleet and sail around to the front, and then—"

"Well? And then—*what?*" Angar Zend demanded.

A stern light shone in Redbeard's eyes, and for a moment a certain grim nobility came over him. His voice dropped to low tones.

"And then, my lads, we ram the *Red Wolf* amidships, and sink her with all hands," he said quietly. "Even if it means the death of all of us. Which I think it will . . ."

They looked at one another in silence.

*

SUDDENLY, Barim Redbeard stiffened and his bronzed features went pale. He had turned from Charn Thovis and Angar Zend, and his gaze had swept the nearby beaches of Ptartha past which they were sailing in the rear of the great fleet. An expression of utter astonishment flickered across his features.

"Now sink me for a lubber," he gasped. "Father Gorm Almighty! It—cannot—*be!*"

"What's the matter, Captain?" Charn Thovis asked. His eyes searched the beaches that lay across the sparkling blue waves of the Gulf, but he could see nothing untoward, and said as much.

"Of course ye can't, lad, being but a lubber. It takes the keen eyes of an ol' sea hawk the likes o' Barim Redbeard, used to squintin' against the sun—Zend, Zend, you black-avised old rogue, give me the glass. The glass, man , or I'll keel-haul ye!"

He made a fierce, urgent gesture at the battered brass-bound spyglass thrust through the sash that the mate wore about his lean middle. Blinking puzzledly at Charn Thovis, the little mate took out the glass and offered it to Captain Redbeard, who all but snatched it from his hand in his hurry to clap the glass against his right eye.

"That little cove there . . . Gods of Sea and Sky, can it *be?*"

For a long, tense moment he glared through the extended glass at the small cove that lay only a little ways from the base of the promontory whereon was builded Tarakus. Then he snatched the glass away.

"It *is,* by the Eleven Scarlet Hells! Ahoy, Minga!" he bellowed to a slant-eyed Cadornyana aloft in the rigging. "*Minga,* you yellow dog! Break out the signal flags—inform Kashtar aboard the *Red Wolf* that *Scimitar* has—has sprung a leak below her waterline and must draw in to shore for a bit to patch 'er up. Tell the rogue we'll catch up with the main body o' the fleet in an hour—hurry, blast you!"

"He's gone mad, mad I say!" Angar Zend gawped. "We've no leak in the bloomin' ship, I'd stake me life on it!"

"*Hah!*" Barim Redbeard snorted, grinning hugely. "Mad, is it? Mad, am I?" He thrust the spyglass into the hands of Angar Zend with a lusty roar. "Clap yer eye to that glass and point 'er at yonder cove, you black rogue, and *then* tell me if I be mad or sane!"

For a long moment, the black-whiskered little mate

peered through the spyglass, and then he stiffened and his jaw dropped in sheer astonishment.

"Great . . . Gods . . . above!" he gasped, while Barim Redbeard chuckled thunderously, exchanging huge winks with the mystified Charn Thovis.

Then Angar Zend thrust the spyglass back into the sash about his middle, turned on his heel and strode smartly to the mid-ship rail. He cocked one eye aloft to see that Minga had completed his exchange of signals with the flagship of the fleet and learned from the wave of Minga's arm that permission to beach had been received. Then he glared fiercely below to where Thangmar, the grinning blond Kodanga giant, was at the wheel.

"Ho, Thangmar, you yellow-haired savage!" the little mate bellowed in an amazingly deep voice. "About ship, you great rogue, ten points to yer starboard bow . . . quick now, look alive . . . heave to in that little cove we just be passin'—quick, you great savage!"

And the *Scimitar* faltered, lost speed, and curved away from the main bulk of the armada and was lost behind.

The young Patangan chanthar, Charn Thovis, was still mystified at this baffling maneuver. But as the lean black hull of Redbeard's ship entered the little cove and he got a good look at the curve of jungle-clad beach, he understood.

And a vast and thrilling joy went through him. His eyes, of a sudden, filled with tears, and deep in his heart he gave profound thanks to the Nineteen Gods Who Watch Over The World . . .

CHAPTER 12:

WHEN COMRADES MEET

Thus through the pathless jungle way,
Whose thousand perils had he passed,
Came Thongor at the dawn of day,
When long-lost comrades meet at last.

—Thongor's Saga, Stave XIX

AS Thongor stepped through the edges of the jungle to look upon the city of Tarakus where it rose black and grim against the flame of the morning sky—the dark figure of a lithe fighting-man suddenly appeared in his path. The quick eyes of the Barbarian caught the cold glitter of steel as the needle-blade of a naked rapier in the hands of his unknown opponent flashed for his unshielded heart.

Swift as a striking cobra his hand flew to the hilt of the great Valkarthan broadsword that lay against his thigh. In a blur of motion he whipped the long blade from its scabbard, in a hiss of steel rasping against leather, and blocked the darting point that strove for his naked flesh.

Steel rang against steel, and the blade of the other was torn from his grip and went spinning into the thick leaves that lay to either side.

His opponent sprang back, reaching for a dirk. As he did so, in stepping back he permitted the faint red glare of dawn to paint his features, and Thongor started, then laughed.

"*Belarba,* Karm Karvus, would you cut down an old comrade?"

The Prince of Tsargol—for of course it was he—staggered with amazement and paled at the thought of what he had attempted to do. He all but rubbed his eyes, staring open-mouthed at this incredible figure that had melted out of the darkness of the jungle path before him like some apparition conjured up by a wizard's rune.

"Thongor! Is it you! Now, by all the Gods," he swore delightedly, "well-met! I had not thought to find you within half a hundred leagues of this place . . ."

They clasped hands, grinning with relief and joy in this most timely and fortunate of meetings.

"As for myself, Karm Karvus, I had hardly thought to see you alive in this world," Thongor replied gravely, "for few men escape whole from the clutches of the Red Wolf of Tarakus. But who is this young woman who companions you?"

"This is the Princess Yian of Cadorna, daughter of Prince Kazan, Lord of that city, and my fellow-prisoner. We have just completed our escape from the Pirate City, and had thought that we would have to tramp many leagues through the jungles of Ptartha before we found a friend. Princess, may I present to you the Lord Thongor, Prince of Patanga and Lord of the Six Cities?"

As Karm Karvus went to retrieve his sword and Thongor bowed over her hand, the Cadornyana girl stared at him wide-eyed with astonishment. Much had she heard of the fabulous and heroic exploits of the mighty Warrior of the West, of the greatness of his golden Empire and the splendor of his court. Could this wild ruffian, this broad-shouldered barbarian in plain warrior's harness, his bare chest and arms slashed with half-healed wounds and black with dried mud, be the glorious Warrior of the West, the tale of whose epic adventures had reached even the far-off city of her birth?

"I shall not waste time by asking how in the world we come to meet you here amidst the jungles of Ptartha," Karm Karvus laughed, "for time is precious. I presume you have moored your airboat nearby and have stepped forth to reconnoitre—we must hasten back to Patanga without delay, Thongor, for this very dawn Kashtar Red Wolf and all his corsairs set sail to raise war against the City of the Flame, armed with the terror of the Gray Death—that very ray of madness that struck down my trireme upon the high seas!"

The light faded from Thongor's dark impassive face and his strange gold eyes went grim and bleak.

"This is dark news indeed, Karm Karvus," he growled. "For on foot and alone have I hewn my path through leagues of jungle to this place, and I have no airboat to hand."

"No? But—how come you here?"

"Aboard the *Scimitar,* a corsair galley out of Tarakus whose captain, Barim Redbeard, is my friend and fellow-countryman. Alas, a sea monster attacked the vessel on our second day out of Patanga and in the confusion I was swept overboard and found myself half-drowned but still alive on the beaches of Ptartha. From thence I have made my way on foot and by raft down Amadon the Jungle River. Where the *Scimitar* may be, and what hath happened to my pirate friends since I took my rather hasty and precipitous departure from their decks, I cannot know. You say the fleet is sailing for Patanga even now?"

"Aye," Karm Karvus nodded. "Unless some timely accident has intervened to cause a change of plan."

Thongor nodded to his right. "Let us see. The beaches of the Gulf lie only a few yards in that direction; come!" And without another word the giant Barbarian turned on his heel and was swallowed up in the thick greenery. Karm Karvus and the girl he had rescued from the clutches of the pirates followed his broad shoulders. Through the dawn-lit jungles they went, emerging at length into the full glory of morning.

Here a small cove met their eyes. A narrow crescent of beach, washed by the sparkling blue waves, separated the looming wall of the green jungles and the glittering expanse of the mighty Gulf.

Shielding his eyes from the blaze of sun upon the dancing waves, Thongor peered out into the Gulf. And it was even as Karm Karvus had said: he could see the billowing sails, the glittering prows, the lean black hulls of a tremendous fleet of ships. They were sailing directly north to the head of the Gulf, where the Twin Rivers of the Ysar and the Saan emptied into the Gulf. Between the mouths of these two rivers, on a narrow spit of land, rose the great City of the Flame.

Karm Karvus and Yian of Cadorna came up to where Thongor stood, arms folded upon his great chest, staring silently out across the waves as rank on rank of ships sailed past to bring red war and the Gray Death to his kingdom.

"Would to Gorm that I did indeed have an airboat moored nearby," Thongor grunted. "In my folly, I feared an airboat might be seen if it approached too closely to the walls of Tarakus—so I shipped instead with Barim Redbeard and his men, who, being themselves Tarakans, could bring me directly into the Pirate City itself without arousing suspicion . . ."

"What can we do?" demanded Karm Karvus helplessly.

Thongor shrugged.

"That is still to be seen," he growled. "We yet live, and while we live, we may hope. There is clearly no way by which we may come to Patanga before the pirate fleet, so there is no use in mourning our inability to do so. Your own city of Tsargol lies at least two days by sea from here . . . Pelorm is far nearer, and as it is a city of the Empire we can find friends there, and a contingent of airboats as well."

"Dense jungles lie between Tarakus and Pelorm," Karm Karvus observed. Again, Thongor shrugged.

"As I have just come through them alone, they are not impassable," he observed. "And now we are three. I have my own broadsword and I see you wear a Tsargolian rapier. while the Princess may take your dirk. The three of us shall travel no slower than one, I trust, and against the fearsome predators that infest the jungles of Ptartha, three blades should prove far better than one. I suggest we waste no time, but begin our journey at once . . ."

Yian, who had been staring out to sea, sudden stifled a small cry and laid her slim hand on Thongor's forearm.

"What is it?"

"That ship . . . look, Lord Thongor, one of the pirates is turning aside from the main mass of the fleet and seems to be sailing directly for this cove wherein we stand!"

Thongor narrowed his eyes against the glare, and saw that the girl had spoken truth. One lean-hulled galley was coming directly for them, and swiftly, its brass-beaked brow slicing through the sparkling waves.

He rumbled a primal challenge deep in his chest, and his eyes flashed. Could their small figures have been glimpsed from aboard one of the passing ships of the Tarakan fleet? Indeed, it was not at all impossible. Seamen have keen eyes, and a spyglass would doubtless reveal them . . .

"Had we not best be gone, then?" Karm Karvus suggested. "They may have seen us, but we can be quite some distance away before they beach . . . and surely they would not attempt to follow us on foot through the trackless jungles?"

"You are right," Thongor grunted. "And yet . . ."

"And yet—what?" asked the Tsargolian.

"And yet . . . there is something about that ship that seems . . . familiar." Thongor mused. His keen eyes searched the on-coming corsair galley. For there was indeed something very familiar about that long, low, rakish black hull, that brass-beaked dragon prow, that spread of scarlet sails . . . and then it struck him!

Tossing back his lion's mane of coarse black hair, he broke into laughter. Karm Karvus stared at him as if he had suddenly gone mad before their very eyes. Yian frowned in puzzlement and stole a bit closer to the gallant Tsargolian as if for protection.

Thongor turned to grin at them.

"No, my friends, I have not lost my reason," he chuckled. "But this would seem indeed the day for old, long-parted friends to meet again—for yonder black galley is none other than the *Scimitar,* and unless mine eyes have lost their wonted keenness, I think I can even see the burning red whiskers of Barim Redbeard himself upon the quarterdeck, aye, and young Charn Thovis, too!"

*

IT was somewhat less than an hour later when the *Scimitar* under full sail came scudding up the wind to rejoin the last rank of the pirate armada, her signal flags reporting the leak repaired and her hull sound once more. And all that day she sailed quietly in her place as the mighty armada paced the length of the Gulf, league after shining league falling away to the stern, lost in the boiling wake of the great armada.

Very great had been the rejoicing aboard the *Scimitar* when Minga and Thangmar returned from the cove, bearing Thongor of Valkarth, Karm Karvus of Tsargol, and the Princess Yian of Cadorna in the longboat. When Thongor climbed up over the rail and waved one mighty hand in salute to the grinning faces that greeted him, a man-throated roar of welcome arose from the men of the pirate crew.

Barim Redbeard was the first to thump him on the back, clearing his throat and fiercely blinking back the tears. He had thought Thongor long since dead and at the bottom of the Gulf; never had he thought to see the mighty Valkarthan alive on this side of the Shadow Gates that divide the Lands of the Living from the dim and illusory Country of the Dead. Indeed, he had bitterly castigated himself for a fancied guilt in Thongor's tragic fall. But here, by some incredible miracle, was the Lord of the West, hale and hearty and—alive!

"Now, Black Hawk, by Gorm, Shastadian and Lady Tiandra!" he roared, clapping Thongor's shoulder with a powerful blow that would have sent a lesser man head over heels into the rowing benches. "Gorm, and All Gods! Alive, eh? Well, Gorm! I—I should have known it takes a lot to kill a Northlanderman!"

Thongor returned his greetings, and those of fat Blay and grinning Thangmar, dour Durgan, smiling Minga, and the rest of his friends aboard the pirate galley. Charn Thovis was overcome with the surprise of finding his Lord alive, and stammered inarticulate words of greeting.

Thongor made Karm Karvus and the Princess of Cadorna known to Captain Barim and the men; then, turning to the master of the *Scimitar,* he said:

"Somewhat later we must exchange an account of all that has happened to us since we were parted, but for now, Redbeard, I trust your galley is well stocked? For I have been hacking my way through the jungles and I find myself in possession of a hearty appetite . . . would there be such a thing as a good big steak aboard this ship, and perhaps a bottle or two of wine?"

Karm Karvus laughed. "I have never known you when you were not thinking of filling your belly!"

Thongor grinned and shrugged.

"If I don't think of it, who will? Besides, adventuring is hungry work . . ."

*

SOME hours later, washed, clad in fresh garments and well fed, Thongor, Karm Karvus and Yian of Cadorna met with Barim Redbeard and Charn Thovis in the great cabin to plan their future moves.

They had each told of their adventures, and Thongor's grim face was impassive as he heard of the terrible powers of the Lamp of Madness, and of Kashtar's plan to use it against Patanga.

" 'Tis a pity we know so little about the plans of the Red Wolf," he growled. "Surely he has some clever scheme in mind . . . I cannot believe he intends to simply sail into the harbor of Patanga in broad daylight . . ."

"Perhaps, Lord, he will time his approach so as to enter the harbor under the cover of darkness," Charn Thovis suggested. "For, as you say, 'twould be foolhardy in the extreme for him to assault Patanga in the full light of day. The Air Guard of Thom Pervis would sight the approach of the fleet long in advance, and the City of the Flame would be alert and in arms by the time the pirate armada arrived."

"Trust that scarlet-clad devil to have some clever scheme in mind," Redbeard growled. "As for myself, Black Hawk, I can think of no better way to frustrate his plans than by the method I told ye . . . to circle the main body of the fleet by darkness o' night, and ram and sink the *Red Wolf*, drowning this Kashtar, his Gray Magician and their hellish weapon under the waters of the Gulf . . . 'tis a risky scheme, and could easily go awry, and it might well sink the old *Scimitar* as well, but flay me if I can think of a better!"

Thongor mused, his strange gold eyes brooding under scowling black brows.

"I agree, Redbeard. Patanga will have an excellent chance to defend herself if we can disable the Gray Death, and I can see no more certain way than that you suggest. Let us prepare for the coming of darkness, and strike when midnight is near and the watchmen in the rigging will be less vigilant . . ."

On this decision the council adjourned. Charn Thovis and Karm Karvus took a last turn around the deck, before going below to sleep so as to be well rested when nightfall came and their plan of action would begin.

"Think you it will work, Prince? Redbeard's plan, I mean?" asked the young chanthar.

The Lord of Tsargol shrugged.

"I cannot say, Charn Thovis. It seems like desperate folly to me . . . but desperate men must sometimes take foolish chances, when all else fails. I like not to endanger the life of the Princess of Cadorna. And it seems we run a very great risk of being seen from another ship as we try to skirt the main body of the fleet . . . but Gorm help me, I can see no better way. Can you?"

Charn Thovis shook his head. Then, peering at the bright sky, he smiled grimly.

"May the Nineteen Gods send us a dark and moonless night," he said quietly.

"I will join you in that wish. And now for my bunk and a few hours of sleep before the night's grim business begins . . ."

They went below, the brave young warrior and the gallant Prince. And the *Scimitar* sailed on across the blue waves of the mighty Gulf, amidst the mighty fleet of the pirates of Tarakus. Night would come all too soon, and no man of them could guess the outcome of the desperate struggle that lay ahead for them all.

CHAPTER 13:

MAGIC MIST

Sometimes it chances in the ways of war, and whether it be but a grim jest of the Gods or a trick of mocking Fate no man can say, that the cunning of one foe plays into the very hands of his enemy.

—The Scarlet Edda

ALL that day the armada of Tarakus sailed up the shining waters of the Gulf of Patanga. Kashtar had instructed his captains to seek the very center of the channel. For the Patangan Gulf was broad and a fleet that rode in the midway between either shore had small chances of being sighted even by keen-eyed and vigilant watchmen in the ports along the coasts.

Their only genuine risk of discovery lay in a chance merchant ship. In case they were sighted by such a craft, Kashtar had given forth commands to board and sink the vessel on the instant, rather than giving it a chance to escape and spread the alarm. But, as the luck of the pirates would have it, no single ship came their way. These were the days of the stormy months that straddled the year halfway between late fall and the beginnings of winter: strong winds blew down from the Mountains of Mommur to the North, and the waters were choppy and hazardous, with sudden squalls and unexpected lightning storms that broke without warning. Few merchant captains dared risk craft, crew and cargo at such a chancy time of year. Hence they sailed north all that day unseen.

Aedir the Sun-god declined slowly, hour by hour, in the West, until at length the azure sky darkened gradually with film on film of deepening gloom, while the horizon of the West became a glorious furnace of crimson and gold.

They had made splendid time up the Gulf, and would reach the harbor of Patanga perhaps before the coming of dawn. Thongor was at a loss to explain the unusual swiftness of their passage, for when he had sailed forth from Patanga aboard the *Scimitar,* the voyage south to Tarakus had taken much longer. But his grim jaw tightened and his gold eyes burned with inscrutable fires: when wizards go forth to war, the ordinary laws of Space and Time are sometimes set aside. Yes, it was doubtless the dark work of that devil Belshathla! The last of the Gray Magicians of Nianga had doubtless eased their sea-passage with the cunning skills of his demon-wrested arts.

As night came down on dark and shadowy wings across the far edges of the world, the men of the *Scimitar* prepared them for their great battle. The silent decks were crowded with hard-faced men, and the hand of every sailor held naked steel. Some were armed with the slim rapiers of Tsargol or the wicked cutlasses of Tarakus, others with the curved sabres of Cadorna, or the straight-bladed longswords of Patanga. Sash and belt and harness bristled with dirk and dagger. The archers were ready to ascend into the rigging at the command, and from high perches aloft they would send a barbed rain of feathered death whistling down to sweep the decks of the *Red Wolf* with swift shafts.

Barim Redbeard had donned a burnished breastplate of bright steel, and a horned steel helm, and glittering greaves shod his booted legs. So that the mirror-like cuirass would not catch and flash forth a vagrant glimmer of light, to catch a wary eye aboard some near ship, he had robed himself in a surcoat of dark wool that concealed the steel armor. The glittering helm he hid beneath a turban-like affair of dark cloth wound about his brows. His great battle-axe hung from its baldric which was slung across his chest and shoulders on the outside of the long robe, so that its hilt would be ready to hand when need came.

Thongor was stripped to a plain warrior's harness of black leather, set with studs of iron. No badge or medallion of precious metals displayed his rank; no jewels flashed at collar or girdle or scabbard. The great Lord of the West, the Sarkon of the Empire of the Six Cities, went into battle clad like any common warrior of savage Valkarth.

Charn Thovis, too, wore no badge or insignia of his noble rank, but was clothed like a simple warrior. His black harness revealed his lithe and supple body, that of a trim young fighting man. But in contrast with the great Barbarian who stood next to him, the young chanthar seemed insignificant. For Thongor towered over him, aye, and over all the seamen that stood near; thewed like some savage gladiator of the Gods was Thongor, with the broad shoulders, the deep chest, the long and powerfully-muscled arms of a mighty champion. His coarse mane of thick hair was held back from his scowling brows by a band of unadorned leather. The massy hilt of Sarkozan lay near his strong hand. His great chest rose and fell with deep, quiet breathing. His face was dark and expressionless, but his eyes blazed with golden fire like the burning orbs of a lion in its kingly wrath.

Aye, Thongor was ready to do battle to save his city . . .

The crew of the *Scimitar* had massed between decks, waiting for darkness to fall. Here were they well concealed from sight, for ahead and behind the raised decks of forecastle and aft sheltered them from observation. High mantlets rose above the benches of the oarsmen, serving to shelter the rowers from arrows in case of assault, and this high wooden wall cast the low deck into deep gloom and helped hide them from any eye. But the chances that they would be seen were very slight, as the *Scimitar* rode far to one side and in the very last rank of the armada of Tarakus. There were no corsair galleys behind to observe them, and none lay to starboard, where the dully gleaming waters of the Gulf fell away to the forested coasts of northern Ptartha.

As the Sun flared crimson in the West, as the world darkened around them, they waited silently for the fall of night and the desperate battle that lay ahead.

*

BARIM Redbeard growled a curse and glowered at the star-gemmed sky. The fortune of the Gods, it would seem, was not with them this night, and the prayers of Karm Karvus and Charn Thovis had not been heard in Paradise.

For the great golden Moon of old Lemuria rose slowly up over the edges of the earth to flood the dark sky, the darker land, and the gleaming sea, with her pallid and silken light.

Barim knew that his chances of withdrawing from the body of the fleet without being seen were now very much lessened by this moonrise. For Illana the Moon Lady showed the full splendor of her shining face this night, and torrents of silver fell across the decks and glittered, flashing, on a thousand dancing waves. It was as if they sailed through a mirror of silver flame, and against the brilliantly illuminated waters of the moonlit Gulf the low black mass of the *Scimitar* would be all too distinctly visible.

Growling barbarous oaths, he chewed fiercely on his mustaches, eyeing the flashing waters about them. Mayhap, in an hour or two, the Moon would hide her golden face behind thick clouds, for the winds of this cold month of Zorah were at work far above the world, and their swift and viewless wings had built tall castles of dark clouds athwart the West.

But against the hopes of this eventuality, he could not wait. Soon, an hour or two, in the very deep of night, he must be about it, and the galley *Scimitar* must detach herself from amongst the ranks of the pirate ships to glide far to the East, up and around the main body of the fleet, so as to strike at the *Red Wolf* where it sailed, as the flagship of the armada, in the foremost rank. And could he do this, unobserved? Would not the watchful eye of some guard stationed high at the masthead of a nearby ship see the black hull of the *Scimitar* cutting through the bright and silvery waves? Alas, it was all too possible. But he must risk the chance of discovery, for there was no other way. Ere dawn shone crimson in the East, the harbor of Patanga would heave into view and the invasion would begin . . .

Cursing and grumbling, Barim Redbeard strode his deck angrily, fiercely demanding of his Gods a thick cover of clouds that the shining face of the Moon might be hidden thereby, and her bright radiance quenched in gloom.

*

AND at this same moment, on the decks of the *Red Wolf* far to the front of the fleet, Kashtar himself was snarling curses at the shining glory of the Moon. Well did he know that the vigilant flying boats of the Air Guard of Patanga circled tirelessly through the night skies above the City of the Flame, and well was he aware how far out into the Gulf their alert pilots could see from so great a height. He, too, wished for cloudy darkness and the cover of night, so that the bulk of his fleet might creep well within the harbor wall of Patanga before the inevitable alarm aroused the fighting men of the city.

But, unlike the captain of the *Scimitar,* the master of the *Red Wolf* had a wizard aboard his ship—and no mere warlock whose abilities were limited to the mixing of philtres or the casting of a minor curse, but one of the mightiest adepts of the Secret Science then alive upon the bosom of the Earth, Belshathla, the last of the Gray Magicians of God-cursed and demon-haunted Nianga, armed with the hellish lore of a lost age of sorcery and science.

And the cunning of Belshathla had taken well into account the need for a secret and unobserved approach to the City of the Flame. For days he had studied the problem, searching through the hieroglyphic pages of age-old tomes of elder magic his hands had rescued from the dark sands of the Gray Barrens and from the oblivion of lost aeons.

There was a mighty spell by which the ships of Tarakus could be rendered invisible to the eyes of men . . . but this spell involved the use of powerful magnetic fields and the bending and twisting awry of the very waves of light themselves, and over water this Operation of the Art could not be accomplished.

The crumbling pages of the ancient books of sorcery also held a vast and terrible formula whereby the minds of men could be made insensible to the approach of many ships . . . this formula, alas, required the skills of nine high adepts of the Secret Science, whose combined strength of will was needed to beguile the brains of so many warriors as might well be watching the waters of the Gulf from the harbor front or guard towers or frowning walls of Patanga, or from the ever-circling airboats of Thom Pervis. And Belshathla was the only adept of his School alive on earth in this age; save for him alone the grim sciences of Nianga were unknown. So this Operation, too, he was forced to pass over in his search.

But the old grimoires held a third method he might employ to render the invasion fleet hidden from the watchful sentinels of Patanga.

This Operation involved the conjuring up of Yathlabnazoor the Demon of the Mists, who could be forced by potent talismans to enshroud the entire Tarakan fleet with his airy cloak of insubstantial vapor, thus concealing the armada from every eye. For to ordinary mortals, whose gaze could not penetrate the gray robes of Yathlabnazoor, 'twould seem but a mighty and impenetrable bank of fog. This magical Operation he set about performing . . . and thus, in his ignorance, he veiled behind the symbolic terminology of Elder Magic a simple scientific experiment which utilized an understanding of the forces of nature, and was not really built upon the Shadowy Lords of Chaos at all. But since Belshathla would get the result he wanted, it did not really matter whether he worked through science or sorcery; the result was the same.

A curious instrument was erected on the foredeck of the corsair flagship. A tall shaft of pure copper rose like a slender mast into the clear moonlight, and at its base a mysterious mechanism glittered, heavy insulated coils writhing about the housing of a powerful transformer. As Belshathla bent over the ominous shape of the instrument, muttering spells and chanting a rune to the Demon of the Mists, he set the machinery into action. Even his well-trained mind but dimly comprehended the nature of the Operation he had set into motion, and to his brilliant but deranged mentality, cloaked as it was in ancient superstition, the positive and negative fields of a powerful electrical generator were invisible Spirits of Power trapped within the core of the heavy transformer, and the crackling blue fire of the electrical discharge that fell in long sparks from the copper antenna, as the current built up these fields, were mindless but potent Elementals from Sithya the Dominion of the Fire Spirits. The metallic stench of ozone that wafted about him was, to his nostrils, the sulphur and brimstone of the Ultimate Pit, and he reveled in the powers that lay, chained and ready, under his trembling hand.

Gradually, droplets of water vapor began to condense out of the thin cold air about him till all the deck was slick and shiny with a queer dew. Blue fire crackled and hummed from the copper conductors; the power coils throbbed like the beating of a giant's heart, and, as the opposed fields of force were projected farther and farther into the night air about the fleet, ever greater volumes of damp vapor condensed into being, until at last the flagship was wreathed in gray billows of heavy mist. With magical swiftness this flowing wall of fog enveloped rank after rank of the moving ships, until the entire armada was totally enveloped in a tremendous cloud. In the elusive moonlight the ships loomed like dark phantoms through the fog, but from any considerable distance even the dark silhouettes were lost to sight behind the mists of enchantment.

And on the quarterdeck of the *Scimitar*, Barim Redbeard gasped with awe as the uncanny mists flowed into being about the fleet. Signal lamps flaring from the rear of the flagship had passed the word down the line that the

Gray Magician was shrouding their passage behind impenetrable mists of magic, so the pirates of the other vessels would not panic in their ignorance.

Then his awe gave way to mirth, and Redbeard broke into peals of laughter. What a grim jest, if the very methods whereby Belshathla sought to protect them from discovery, were to prove an agent that permitted the *Scimitar* to fall upon the flagship unobserved, and take it by surprise!

CHAPTER 14:

NAKED STEEL

Unseen and silent as a ghost
The galley clove the waves and came
To where the Red Wolf *led the host*
Against the City of the Flame . . .

—Thongor's Saga, Stave XIX

NOW that the vast armada of the corsairs moved through the still night, cloaked in a veil of magic mists, Barim Redbeard was free to strike for the kill.

They had thought to wait until the hour of midnight, when the greater number of the pirates aboard the nearby ships would perchance be deep in slumber, hence to make their strike under the smallest danger of observation. But now the enchantments of the Gray Magician made it no longer necessary for the sea wolves of Barim Redbeard to delay the hour. They would strike—now!

A ghost-ship gliding through the phantasmal fog, the lean black galley slid from her place in the last rank of the armada, and fell aside to starboard. All about the decks, gray streamers of the clammy fog swirled like the impalpable draperies that clad the skeletal limbs of the spirits of the dead. Queer tricks were played by fog and wind: leering mask-like faces appeared out of the sliding film of fog, eye-holes and maw but gaping rents in the mist, torn by unpredictable gusts of wind.

Long coils of mist drifted out, like reaching arms, as if

to seize the sailors clustered on the mid-ship deck. Although they knew the nature of the mist to be Belshathla's demon sorcery, this did but little to allay the superstitious fears that arose in many of the seamen. Many a grim-faced warrior, standing with naked steel in his hands, ready to face death upon the signal, felt his heart go cold and the chill sweat of terror bedew his brow. Even fat old Blay felt the clammy fingers of fear clutch about his stout old heart as he blinked and gawped at the gliding phantasmal forms that flickered eerily across the deck, borne on the invisible wings of the wind.

Near him, laconic one-eyed Durgan paled and swore under his breath, and the grinning blond Kodanga giant, Thangmar, grinned no more, but clutched the little green paste idol of his tribal god suspended by a leathern thong about his thick-corded throat. Aye, even the nine-foot-tall Blue Nomad, Roegir, muttered a counter charm to ward off the Demon of the Mists.

Then suddenly they were clear of the fogbank, and sailing out across open water. Dancing waves were glittering with the silvery path of Illana the Moon Lady who rode serene and glorious against the bosom of the night. As the last gray tendrils of mist were whipped away from the decks of the *Scimitar,* many a hardy seamen there was who felt his spirits rise and who breathed a bit easier.

Barim commanded his men to clap on every foot of canvas the masts would bear, for he must outrace the armada and circle it, approaching from the front. Wind boomed in the scarlet sails, and the brass-beaked dragon prow of the corsair galley cut through the moon-silvered waters at an ever more rapid pace. Now rank on rank of the great armada was falling away behind them as they strove to out-distance the fleet.

Not yet were the soaring towers and mighty battlements of Patanga visible on the horizon. But it would not be long before the king-city of the Empire would heave into view . . .

*

ERE long the master seamanship of Barim Redbeard had proven itself, and they had circled the great mass of ships and now rode even with the foremost rank of the attack force.

Now with great care and craft and subtlety, the captain guided the *Scimitar* within the moving mass of magic mist.

Like fog-cloaked phantoms, the dark shapes of ships loomed up about them through the gray gloom. Red and green, like the burning eyes of demons, the ship lights burned dimly through the fog. No light showing, all but invisible in the swirling vapors, the *Scimitar* wove like a sea serpent through the line of ships until at length the unmistakable silhouette of the great flagship, the *Red Wolf* itself, loomed up before their bows.

With great care, Redbeard maneuvered his rudder and trimmed his sail, until at last he rode steady, directly to starboard of Kashtar's flagship.

And now it was Thongor's turn to take action.

The mighty Warrior of the West had devised an alternate plan of attack. Rather than gamble everything on a single throw of the dice, he decided to try a different scheme. Were the *Scimitar* to attempt to ram and sink Kashtar's ship—and fail—they would be left utterly helpless. Thus he grimly commanded Barim Redbeard to hold his helm in readiness, while Thongor gambled his life on his fighting skill. He and young Charn Thovis would dive overboard and swim the hundred yards or less that lay between the two ships; rising from the waves, they would attempt to wreck the Lamp of Madness—aye, and that weird instrument which had conjured up the magic mists, as well, whose crackling aura of blue fire could be seen yonder across the fog-wreathed waters—and if perchance they should fail to do so within a given time, then Thongor commanded that Redbeard should bring about the *Scimitar* and ram the *Red Wolf* amidships.

Growling at this, the pirate captain grudgingly agreed. To his simple way of thought, direct action was the only route to success, but the Lord of the West was his Lord as well, and he had no recourse but to submit. Far rather would he have preferred to send his brass-beaked prow crashing like a brazen ram deep into the timbers of the flagship's hull, and sweep aboard the decks of the enemy with a naked cutlass flashing in his hand. But he would yield to Thongor in this.

Thus, when the ship was positioned and all was ready, Thongor stripped off his black cloak and removed his heavy sea-boots so that they should not encumber him as he swam. The mighty Valkarthan broadsword swung at his thigh, and he knew that down there in the cold waves of the Gulf the long scabbard might well entangle his legs and hamper his movements, so he borrowed a baldric from Barim Redbeard and slid the glittering length of Sarkozan into this, slinging the baldric over his chest and adjusting the scabbard so that the sword would hang down between his shoulders, giving his arms and legs free play.

Then, making certain that the young chanthar, Charn Thovis, was similarly accoutered, he wasted no time in lingering farewells, but sprang to the top of the mantlets that shielded the rowing benches. For a moment he loomed there above them, astride the wooden shield. The next moment he raised one hand in farewell, and vanished over the side. Charn Thovis followed him. The two warriors clambered down the curving hull of the galley and slid silently into the dark cold waters.

The stinging shock of the chilly waves struck new vigor into Thongor's mighty thews. Setting his heels against the waterline of the *Scimitar,* the Valkarthan kicked out and propelled himself away from the vessel. His great shoulders rose and fell, his long powerful arms clove through the waves, as he swam towards the dim hulk of the pirate flagship that towered up, a vague and fog-wreathed silhouette, across the dark waters.

It was not as difficult to see as Thongor had imagined. The barrier of magic mist did not extend down all the way to the surface of the water, but ended a foot or two above the waves. Thongor had grimly taken into account the possibility that the flagship would be invisible to him once he was in the waters of the Gulf, so he had securely fixed its position in his mind before going overboard. He was relieved to learn that such was not the case. And it was a distinct relief to know he did not have to worry about swimming the black cold waters, lost.

As he swam towards the hull of the *Red Wolf,* Thongor turned to see how Charn Thovis was doing. The young swordsman was behind him and to his left, following him as he swam. Thongor grinned at his young comrade, white teeth flashing in the murk, and turned his attentions to swimming.

All about them the night was murmurous. The slap and slither of waves against the gliding ships, the creak of the masts, the hollow boom of the sails, the song of the wind in the rigging, the distant sound of voices. Surely, Thongor thought, amidst all this the two of them would make no sound that might attract attention.

After some little time, the hull of the pirate galley rose above them, and Thongor slowed his progress. The Lamp of Madness, Karm Karvus had told him, was erected upon the foredeck of the *Red Wolf*. So he sank underwater and swam about the prow of the ship, coming up before its figurehead.

Reaching up, he caught a hand-hold in the gilt and carven sea monster which adorned the prow, and drew himself dripping from the waves. The prow was carven with heavy scrollwork, which afforded easy hand-holds. Thus the Valkarthan, with Charn Thovis at his heels, climbed to the foredeck without difficulties.

He lifted his brows above the deck-rail and searched the scene before him with burning eyes.

That weird mechanism of twinkling brass and sparkling crystal must be the very Lamp of Madness itself, for it matched the description Karm Karvus had given him of the deadly ray machine in every particular. And there beyond it, before the deck house, that soaring copper antenna wreathed in crackling sparks of blue electric fire, that must be the devil-thing that had caused the enchanted mists to envelop the fleet and hide it from watchful eyes.

Two guards stood before the mind-destroying ray projector with naked steel in their hands, he saw. But the mist mechanism was unguarded . . .

Thongor's head sank down behind the carven work and he crouched there at the prow for a moment, whispering a plan to Charn Thovis. The young noble nodded, and Thongor began the chancey business of climbing around the curve of the hull, clinging to precarious hand- and toe-holds on the outside of the ship, until at length he came to a place somewhat behind the position of the two guards.

Then, silent as a phantom, his mighty figure all but invisible amidst the ghostly fog, the Valkarthan glided up and over the rail. His wet feet crept across the planking as he advanced upon the two unsuspecting guards. As he approached them, a ghostly and silent figure in the gray gloom, his strong fingers closed about the massy hilt of Sarkozan.

With but the faintest whisper of steel against leather, he drew the glistening length of the broadsword free from its scabbard. With naked steel glistening in his hand, he advanced with the soundless tread of a stalking vandar upon the two guards . . .

*

FRONTING upon the Great Plaza that lay at the heart of Patanga, the spires of the Air Citadel ascended into the moonlit skies. The upper works of this citadel were honeycombed with entry ports and hangars, for this towering structure housed the Air Guard of Patanga.

On this cold, windy night in the late fall, the command of the night patrol had fallen to Changan Jal, a senior officer of the Guard. At his desk in the signal tower, he received a flow of reports from the airboats of his patrol as they circled tirelessly above the City of the Flame. With monotonous regularity these reports delivered the identical message: no activity.

Once each night, to relieve the boredom of his administrative duties, Changan Jal liked to go aloft in his sleek command boat, to make an aerial tour of the city himself. And this night, some time before the middle hour, he left his desk and went out on the wind-swept flight deck for his accustomed round.

Anzan Varl, an alert young Otar under his command, would serve this night as his pilot. And the trim little airboat was powered and ready, hovering at the length of its mooring mast. The cold, alert eyes of the older officer softened as they gazed on the sleek lines of the speedy little craft, and lingered approvingly on the powerful electrode of the lightning gun that was built into the pointed prow.

What hath Patanga to fear from any foe, he thought with satisfaction, *with such a flying fleet of vessels to guard her skies?*

Settling the winged silver helm on his close-cropped, graying hair and drawing his flowing blue cloak about him more closely against the cold night wind, the senior commander returned the young Otar's crisp salute and boarded the hovering airboat. Seating himself in the snug little cabin, he held the controls steady while Anzan Varl loosed the mooring lines and took his place in the pilot's chair. Then, in the observer's position, the older officer watched as the Otar took the trim little craft up to the twenty-thousand-foot-level and began a tour of the city.

The night was clear and cold, the wind from the south, with a touch of frost in it. The streets were all but empty in the city below their floating keel, save for an occasional squadron of the Night Watch tramping their rounds.

As the slim airboat curved far above the harbor area, however, the eyes of Changan Jal sharpened and an expression of bafflement crossed his stern features.

"Otar! Take her down to five thousand feet and level off," he ordered. Obediently, the airboat sank to the lower level and steadied in her flight, while the keen eyes of the senior commander searched the peculiar thing he had sighted from aloft.

"What is it, sir?" the pilot inquired.

Changan Jal shrugged thoughtfully.

"Probably nothing, but . . . it *is* odd! That great fogbank rolling in from the Gulf—see? It all but blocks the channel. Odd, to see so heavy a mass of fog on so clear and cold a night as this is . . . and the wind from the south, too! I should have thought any fog would disperse before such gusts."

For a long moment the airboat circled above the harbor area, while the two Air Guards observed the peculiar actions of the mysterious bank of mists. There was something uncanny about that cloud of grayness, something that aroused the suspicions of the senior commander. But nothing that he could name. A formless feeling—almost like an intuition; certainly nothing he could label. Yet it *was* odd . . . for forty years Changan Jal had dwelt in the great City of the Flame that rose here at the head of the Gulf between the Twin Rivers, and never in all that time had he observed fog to act as strangely as this . . .

"Shall I give the signal to alert the patrol?" asked Anzan Varl. His commander rubbed a thoughtful hand across his trim small beard.

"No," he said at last. " 'Tis but a fog, and what's harm in that? The morning sun will disperse it soon enough, I warrant. No, Otar, continue the patrol."

The airboat rapidly ascended to the proper level and continued its circuit of the great city. Changan Jal shrugged, and put aside from his mind the strange action of the mysterious mists.

Still . . . it *was* odd . . .

BOOK FOUR

THE STORM PASSES

"Earth stands ever in peril from the Forces of Darkness, for the legions of Chaos and Old Night wait ever at the portals to the Universe to work destruction and evil against Creation; many and manifold are the means whereby the Dark Powers work for the doom of man, and science and sorcery are the weapons they employ . . . and against such weapons, mortal men have little else wherewith to combat the Darkness . . . but they have courage and strength and faith, and these three be enough to win the victory."

—*The Great Book of Sharajsha the Wizard*

CHAPTER 15:

THE GOLDEN DRAGON

A phantom monstrous in the gloom,
He rose out of the waves to stand
Before the awesome Lamp of Doom,
And naked steel was in his hand.

—Thongor's Saga, Stave XIX

THONGOR was upon the first guard in an instant. He bore him to the deck before his rush, like a charging lion. Before the corsair had time to utter a single cry, the iron hands of the Barbarian had crushed him to silence. And even in the same instant Thongor sprang upon the first guard, Charn Thovis hurled himself upon the second. Bright steel flashed and red blood spurted, and the second watchman sank to the deck without a groan.

Alas, the man Charn Thovis struck down bore a naked cutlass in his hands. And as the steel blade of the young chanthar was driven through the pirate's heart, his muscles leaped in a last convulsion—and the blade fell clattering and clanging to the deck. As luck would have it, the cutlass struck the metallic housing of the base of the Lamp of Madness and the clash of steel on steel rang across the deck like an alarm bell.

Even as Thongor rose from the recumbent body of his kill, the midships watch shouted a query and a whiskered face thrust itself up the top of the stairway that led from the main deck to the raised platform whereon they stood.

"What's the clamor, mates—" the watchman said, but Thongor's flashing sword caught him across the throat and he fell, gurgling, down the stairs to land with a thump and clatter. The alarm was given now, and Thongor and Charn Thovis heard the drum of booted feet pounding up from below.

"I will hold the head of the stair," Thongor growled. "You wreck the ray projector. Swift, now, lad!"

And he swung away to stand at the head of the stair, the great broadsword clenched in his fists. Its bright steel glowed wetly crimson now, and the first pirates who came charging up the stair faltered at this grim and terrible apparition that had melted out of thin air to oppose them.

Up flashed the broadsword—and down it came, ringing in cloven bone—and a second corpse fell dead at the foot of the stair. Snarling like an enraged panther, a black-bearded corsair replaced his fallen mate, cutlass raised to block Thongor's blow. The metallic music of sword against sword rang out, and Thongor was battling furiously.

Little there was in life the great Valkarthan loved more than a good fight—and this was one of the best! His broadsword rose and fell tirelessly, and soon with every sweep the blade left a curve of crimson droplets traced upon the air. Blocking the head of the stair as he did, the Barbarian had the great advantage of height—and a second, in that the maddened pirates could only come at him one at a time. For a short while he killed and killed, sustaining no more than a sabre-cut on his bare thigh and a scratch or two on chest and shoulder.

From the foredeck at his back, where he had left Charn Thovis to wreck the projector, Thongor heard but silence. For some moments he was too heavily engaged in holding the pirates at bay to think much about the queer stillness at his back. But ere long it troubled him, and he cast a glance over his shoulder—

The glowing tip of Belshathla's wand caught his shoulder with a numbing shock that drove Thongor staggering.

A cold electric thrill ran down his right arm from that uncanny blow. And then the great crimson blade of Sarkozan fell from numb and nerveless fingers to ring against the iron studs of the deck. Before Thongor could move or even attempt to shrug off the cold paralysis that gripped him, the pirates fell on him from behind and bore him struggling to the deck while Belshathla stood watching, a cold smile of gloating triumph on his skull-like face.

Thongor caught one quick glance at the sprawled form of Charn Thovis where the youth lay face downward and unmoving before the instrument he had striven to destroy . . . then the tide of brawny bodies crushed him under a smothering weight.

Belshathla had emerged from the deck house in time to

fell Charn Thovis with the touch of his paralyzing wand before the youth had damaged the projector of the mind-destroying ray. Drawn forth perhaps by some occult premonition that danger threatened his beloved mechanisms, the Gray Magician had first struck down the young warrior and then had advanced to deal a numbing blow to Thongor. He had intended to touch the Barbarian at the base of his skull with the weirdly glowing tip of his wand, but Thongor had turned at just the right moment, so that the paralyzing blast struck only his shoulder and not his brain.

Thus the Valkarthan was still fully conscious, and, although his arm tingled from fingertip to shoulder from the surge of uncanny force, he was otherwise unharmed and in possession of his faculties.

Even deprived of the strength of his right arm, he was a formidable opponent. And before they crushed him down under the sheer weight of bodies, his savage blows had hurled several of the corsairs sprawling with broken jaw or shattered ribs. But at last they held him helpless.

"Let me kill the dog now, wizard," one of the pirates spat. His dirty fist held a dagger whose glittering point was suspended above the naked chest of Thongor.

The commotion above had roused Kashtar from his cabin and now the Pirate King gained the foredeck in time to halt this impending blow with a curt word of command.

Reluctantly, the other put aside his blade as the captain of the *Red Wolf* came to stand over Thongor where he lay pinned beneath a mass of panting corsairs. A cold mirthless smile touched the lips of the Lord of Tarakus as he surveyed his captive.

"So the Lord of Patanga has come forth to welcome the guests at his gate!" he purred with a note of feline menace in his silken tones. Thongor grunted and spat.

"Shall we slay him, Lord?" the Gray Magician asked. "It is dangerous to permit him to live, even though a captive. For, although many men have held the Barbarian prisoner ere now, none of them are now alive. He has a way of eluding captivity . . ."

Kashtar shook his head.

"Wizard you may be, but you are also a great fool, you gray dog," he said. "For you would throw away the key that Fate has set within our very grasp! Aye, here's the key that will unlock the gates of Patanga before us . . . think you they will dare oppose us, when we hold a knife at the heart of their Lord and King?"

Belshathla hovered, indecisively, searching for words. His instincts told him that now, while he lay helpless, was the time to slay the dread Warrior of the West. What had they to fear from all the fighting force of the City of the Flame, while the Lamp of Madness was their weapon to employ? And yet, here Kashtar commanded and not Belshathla.

"What shall we do with him, then?"

"Shackle the dog to the prow, so that when we enter Patanga harbor, all his warriors may see their mighty Sark our helpless slave."

Heavy chains were set on Thongor's wrists and ankles, and he was dragged across the deck growling, to be bound at the very prow.

And even as the hand of one burly rogue went forth to lock the shackles—a clear voice rang out across the deck and froze them all motionless.

"Loose the Lord Thongor, or you are all dead men!"

*

KASHTAR spun on his heel, snarling.

And there stood young Charn Thovis at the Lamp of Madness. His paralysis had passed while they had gathered about the great Valkarthan. Finding himself ignored for the moment, the young chanthar had swung the ray projector about on its gimbals until the terrible crystal tube of the weapon was aimed full at the pirate band. With one hand on the throttle of the instrument, he held them all at bay. For every eye could read the truth of his words—he had thrust the dial over into the range of killing intensity, having heard Karm Karvus describe the controls of the magical weapon.

Even Belshathla blenched and recoiled before the ominous glittering crystal snout of the ray projector.

The hands of the pirates fell away, and Thongor stood free, albeit heavy steel chains still dangled from his hands.

"Well done, Charn Thovis," he growled, as he tore

from the hands of his captor the ring of keys. Swiftly he unfastened the chains at his ankles and wrists, and tossed them aside. Stooping, he found the fallen broadsword where it lay in a welter of gore.

None of them saw the grinning pirate who had climbed the foredeck rail behind the deck house and who crept now on silent feet behind the gallant young warrior. It was Duranga Thool, Kashtar's chief lieutenant. He had stood in the darkness of the midship deck below, listening. And now as he heard the young chanthar threaten his captain, he had climbed the rail and now he slunk like a shadow behind Charn Thovis where he stood holding them all at bay.

Suddenly his powerful arms enveloped the young warrior and whirled him away from the controls.

In the same instant, Thongor struck out with his broadsword, felling the pirate who stood nearest to him, striving to cut a path to the Lamp of Madness.

All was howling pandemonium in the next instant.

Belshathla thrust his glowing wand at Thongor but the bronze giant dodged to one side, and cut down another foe.

Kashtar voiced a snarling cry and whipped out his rapier, springing to engage the Valkarthan.

The crowd of pirates surged about Thongor. In every hand naked steel flashed—dirk and dagger, sword and sabre, cutlass and scimitar. Thongor battled like a trapped tiger amidst the howling mob.

At the forward rail, Charn Thovis staggered to his feet—snatched up a sword—and turned to engage Duranga Thool.

Thongor's mighty blade wove a wall of flashing steel about him, as he held off the swords of nine opponents.

Grinning, Duranga Thool beat Charn Thovis back with lusty blows from his cutlass. The pirate chieftain was the taller and the heavier man, and his burly shoulders drove the blade against the youth with telling force. Step by step, Charn Thovis was driven back until at length he stood against the rail and could retreat no further. With every ounce of skill and strength within him, the young warrior strove to keep the edge of that flying blade from his throat.

Now the thud of booted feet came pounding up the stair, as dozens of corsairs came belatedly to join their comrades in the unequal battle against two lone swordsmen.

Thongor had cut down six men. They lay heaped about him like a wall of gory corpses. But the corsairs had ringed him in now, and he must strive with redoubled vigor to hold at bay so many flashing points. Now keen blades were lifted against his unshielded back. Within moments, he knew, the unequal contest would end and he would fall, struck down from behind. Yet still he fought on, and would fight on till the very end.

A moment more, and his spirit would go on its last voyage into the Shadowlands, to dwell forever with the mighty dead who thronged the Hall of Heroes. But he would not go empty-handed before the shining throne of Father Gorm . . . for he would send many of his enemies down into death before his valiant heart beat its last . . .

*

THERE where he stood against the rail, Charn Thovis fell reeling under a shower of blows. At last the heavier blade of Duranga Thool beat his own weapon aside, and his breast was unprotected.

With supernatural clarity the young warrior could see every line in the snarling, grinning face of the pirate as Duranga Thool drew back to plunge his sword through the heart of Charn Thovis. He could see the perspiration that beaded the brows of the pirate, the expression of hatred and triumph stamped on his swarthy features, the blaze of blood-lust in his vicious eyes—

Then, even as he watched, a miraculous change came over the face of Duranga Thool. From a snarling mask of murderous fury it was transformed to blank astonishment. The eyes goggled unbelievingly and the sword, drawn back for the final lunge, went wavering aside.

Charn Thovis knew not the cause of the gap-jawed amazement that had struck the other, but his hand flew to seize this momentary advantage. And in the next instant, with the last dregs of his strength, he had thrust his own sharp rapier through the hairy breast before him.

With gore dribbling from his open mouth, Duranga

Thool fell stone dead at the feet of the young warrior.

And in the next instant, Charn Thovis knew the cause of the astonishment that had frozen the hand of Duranga Thool.

For looming out of the phantasmal mists, the contorted face of a dragon towered above the rail. Light glinted gold from its burnished beak and frowning brow.

In the next instant the deck shuddered under their feet as the brass-beaked dragon prow of the *Scimitar* drove full against the hull of the *Red Wolf*.

The rail came apart in flying fragments. Timbers crunched and squealed as the terrible brass ram came crashing through the side of the corsair flagship. Men fell like toppling ninepins as the *Red Wolf* shook under the impact of the collision.

And in the next moment, flying through the fog, a score of howling warriors came swarming aboard the crippled vessel with swords flashing in their fists. And at their fore towered a roaring giant in steel cuirass and horned helm, wielding a great axe, his fiery beard blazing through the murk.

Barim Redbeard had come at last.

CHAPTER 16:

THE RAY OF MADNESS

Steel rings on steel—an iron song!
We hew our red path through the throng
And with each stroke we break their line—
As drunk with battle as with wine!

—The Battle-Song of the Black Dragons

BARIM REDBEARD had waited as long as he dared before driving his battering prow into the side of the *Red Wolf*. The time allotted to Thongor and Charn Thovis had elapsed, aye, and a bit more, and still the magic mists seethed about the pirate armada. Then, faintly to his ears across the dark waters, came the red music of battle and the mighty Redbeard knew that his friends had been discovered in the work of smashing the devil machines.

The command boomed from his lips and the prow of the *Scimitar* swung for the black hull of the flagship and the great golden dragon-ram at her prow went crashing through a hail of flying timbers as the *Scimitar* clove the *Red Wolf*'s side.

Leaving the command to little Angar Zend, Barim seized a dangling shroud and swung over to board the pirate vessel in the van of his warriors. His boots came crashing down into the astounded face of one of Kashtar's men. The Redbeard landed on the deck and the man whose face had cushioned his fall went reeling back, spitting broken teeth in a welter of splattering blood.

Voicing a lusty challenge, the mighty Redbeard sprang into battle. His weapon of choice for this red business of boarding was a great Belnarthan battleaxe. With this mighty blade, swinging with the savage strength of tireless arms, he cut his way to the center of the deck. At his right the blond Kodangan giant, Thangmar, slew with a scimitar of shining steel; at his left the Rmoahal titan, Roegir, wielded a great broadsword. The three of them, who were the mightiest men and the champions of the *Scimitar*, fought through the howling horde of Kashtar's crew with ease. And at their backs a roaring tide of their comrades followed.

From the foredeck, which loomed up from the swirling mists to his right hand, the keen ears of Barim Redbeard heard the deep booming challenge of the Valkarthan war cry—the call of the Black Hawk tribe. He answered it with the war cry of his own folk, the White Wolf warriors of Belnarth. And, turning, he began to cut a path through snarling men to reach the place where Thongor battled alone, ringed in by the foe.

The flagship of the Tarakan fleet was crammed to the gunwales with fighting men, and the *Scimitar* shipped no more than the ordinary number of her crew. Still, the overwhelming advantage of surprise was on the side of Barim, and he seized on this advantage to the fullest. Wave after wave of his men came swarming over the shattered wreckage of the rail, and in mere instants the decks were alive with battling figures and the roar of yelling men; the shriek of the wounded, the screams of the dying, rang through the fog like a chorus of the damned yowling up from the scarlet hells of the Ultimate Pit.

Chanting a lusty war song of his primitive people, Barim Redbeard carved his way towards the stair that led to the foredeck. His deep-chested anthem boomed above the snarling, yapping chaos that seethed and eddied around him, as he hacked a path to the side of Thongor.

*

BLAY was stout and heavy-built. Not to be unkind, one might as well admit he was—fat. But beneath his wobbling paunch and red, moon-faced exterior there beat the valiant heart of a fighting man. Laying about him lustily with an old cutlass, his girdle bristling with daggers and dirks, his high-topped sea-boots flopping, he must have seemed a ferocious figure as he came whacking through the mists, snorting and wheezing curses.

At his side his old comrade, Durgan, fought. The dour-faced, lean and leathery old pirate used a fine sabre, and he used it with great skill. Bright gems flashed in the hilt of that sabre, and it needed no stretch of the imagination to hazard that once it had slapped against the thigh of some high admiral or noble lord, ere it had fallen as booty into his lean old hand. His one good eye glancing sourly about, the empty socket of the other hidden beneath a black patch that flapped with every sword-stroke, the gaunt old corsair fought with surprising vigor.

Eventually they found themselves at the mainmast. The crowd had somewhat fallen away by now, and many erstwhile members of it lay red and limp underfoot. Leaning on the nicked blade of his battered old cutlass, Blay found a quiet moment to catch his breath and he seized the opportunity thus offered by this momentary lull in the battle to sneak a surreptitious draught from the fat black wine-bottle that hung from his girdle by a thong.

He upended the bottle and let its contents gurgle into his mouth for a spell, until forced to come up for breath. Smacking his lips at the sound of flowing liquor, gaunt old Durgan took it from him and gave it similar employment for a bit.

The tide of battle was swinging their way again, so

Durgan thrust the bottle back into the hands of his wheezing old comrade, who hastily corked it and put it back in its place.

Then, refreshed and stimulated to new efforts, Blay and Durgan returned to their red work of slash and cut and parry and were soon far too busy to feel thirsty.

*

WHEN the *Scimitar* had rammed the flagship of the Tarakan fleet amidships, the shuddering shock and roll of the deck had knocked the men around him from their feet. All but Thongor, who had glimpsed the brass-beaked dragon looming above the rail an instant before she struck.

Thus, as his foes went tumbling to the deck, the Valkarthan took advantage of this brief respite to extricate himself from the circle of his foes. Thrusting the blade of his great Valkarthan broadsword back in the scabbard that was still clipped to the baldric slung across his chest, he sprang up, seized the shrouds, and was up into the rigging in an instant.

From this high vantage, he could see the furious work that Barim Redbeard and his stout-hearted men were wreaking on the stunned and staggering crew of the *Red Wolf*. He grinned at the lusty vigor with which the towering Redbeard cut deeply into the enemy crew. And the roaring seamen that swarmed over the rail, brandishing their cutlasses, and surging into battle behind their mighty chief, delighted his heart.

Cold winds blew about him as he clung to the frost-sheathed rigging. He knew that it must be midnight by now, perhaps later. And he knew that if this was so, they must by now be well within the sight of the flying patrols of Patanga.

Doubtless the airboats had assumed the fogbank, which hid from all eyes the invasion fleet, to be but a harmless mass of mist. Which meant they had given no alarm to the fighting forces of the City of the Flame.

But if Thongor could disable the mist machine now, the fogs would melt away and the alarm would go out to the gallant warriors of Patanga. Hence he determined to take advantage of the distraction afforded by the surprise attack of Barim's crew, to wreck the instrument. From his height, he could see it plainly, even through the swirling film of gray gloom. Blue fire crackled eerily about the slender copper antenna.

Hacking loose a shroud line with his dagger, he released his footing and swung through the fogs directly at the soaring column of blue flame . . .

*

THE warriors of Barim Redbeard had fought their way to the foot of the stairway that led up to the foredeck.

A chance surge of the struggling mass of men had thrust the Redbeard and Thangmar and Roegir away from the stair; hence it was not they but their comrades, Gorchak and Turan and laughing, golden-skinned Minga, who were the first to reach the foot of the ladder.

Howling like wolves, they charged up the stairs to the higher level whereon stood Kashtar and Belshathla and a host of seamen. Charn Thovis was there, too, holding three swords at bay with his own. The young chanthar, who instantly recognized the grinning faces of Barim's men, was happy to step back and catch his breath while they flung themselves forward to engage his opponents in his place.

Suddenly the noisy air thrilled to a weird sound.

A deep-throated humming rose amid the clangor of battle, rising swiftly to a shrill scream that sent crawling terror through the tingling nerves of all who heard it. The vigor of battle faltered, and a lull came, as men turned to see the source of this eerie song.

At the controls of the Lamp of Madness stood Belshathla.

He had swung the instrument about so that its terrible beam could rake the decks below.

His hand rested lightly on the throttle. As yet the deadly ray shone not from the glowing crystal globes. But the engines were engaged, and were he to thrust the throttle home—red raving madness would sweep over the warriors below.

Frozen with horror, the pirates—friend and foe alike—stood motionless. They stared up into the cold glassy eye of the Gray Death as doomed men stare at the unwinking glitter of the headsman's axe as it hangs above their heads.

No one could move or think fast enough to avert the horror that hung over them.

Minga, Turan and Gorchak were too far away, there at the head of the stair.

Only Charn Thovis was upon the foredeck. And he was held back by a wall of swordsmen. He could never cut through them in time.

The glittering crystal eye of the Lamp of Madness glared straight at the figure of Barim Redbeard.

The hand of Belshathla tightened on the lever.

And thrust it home!

CHAPTER 17:

KASHTAR'S DOOM

When danger threatens and doom hangs
hovering on beating wings—strike
with all your strength, and trust in
the mercy of thy Gods, O Warrior!

—The Scarlet Edda

THE paralysis of horror seemed to hold them frozen for long minutes of time, but this was a trick of the mind. Actually, these things occured in but a fraction of a second.

Thongor had already launched himself into the air, to swing across the decks to where the copper antenna of the mist machine loomed like a spire of azure flame.

In mid-flight he glimpsed the Gray Magician at the controls of the Lamp of Madness—his sharp eyes saw that the machine was trained on the midship decks where the bulk of Barim Redbeard's crew was gathered.

It was impossible for him, at this juncture, to alter the direction of his swing. But he seized the hilt of Sarkozan and brought the great broadsword from its sheath with a squeal of rasping leather.

The great blade flashed in the misty air as he swung it

with a desperate surge of strength.

The hissing blade caught Belshathla just below the ear and sheared his head off cleanly.

The wizard's head thudded to the deck and rolled away into a corner of the deck like some great grisly fruit.

Black blood spewed up in a hideous fountain from the severed stump. The headless body lurched drunkenly and fell over. In falling, one shoulder struck the central tube of the ray projector, and it swung aside with a screech of swiveling gimbals.

Now the harsh droning whine had ascended to a shrill maddening whistle. Weird luminance flickered within the hollow globes of polished crystal. From the snout of the projector a dull beam of throbbing colorless light flashed—

But Belshathla's sprawling corpse had knocked the projector askew and the throbbing beam of madness played—not upon the decks of the *Red Wolf,* a-swarm with Barim Redbeard's crew—but upon the shadowy black hulk of the next ship of the armada!

This ship, the *Thurdan Maid,* rode shoulder to shoulder with the flagship of Kashtar.

Only the width of a hundred yards lay between the two corsair galleys. The gray beam flashed across the stretch of cold waters and shone full on the decks of the neighboring vessel.

The crewmen and warriors of the *Thurdan Maid* stood shoulder to shoulder along the starboard rail. They had, some few minutes ago, been startled to hear the crunch of a ship being rammed, the clashing of swords, the hoarse cries of the fallen. Already their captain was putting about to investigate the battle that seemed to be raging aboard the flagship of the fleet. But now a beam of weird gray light played across the crowded decks—and the men of the *Thurdan Maid* went raving mad!

Seamen turned to seaman and cut him down with a sudden flash of unsheathed blade. Shipmate sprang snarling upon shipmate, to slash at his throat with bared teeth, to claw at his eyes with hooked fingers. In an instant the decks of the ship were a screaming maelstrom of homicidal maniacs battling each other like wild beasts.

Standing by the mast, the captain of the *Thurdan Maid*

was caught and bathed in the lambent and colorless radiance that shone from the foredeck of the flagship. Throwing back his head, he roared out a bellow of primal fury and turned upon the bewildered sailor who stood at the wheel. With one terrific stroke of his cutlass the captain disemboweled the seaman. Then he turned away to engage another man, while the dead man slumped before the wheel.

With no hand upon the wheel, it whirled wildly, caught in the currents. The prow of the *Thurdan Maid* came about sharply and the heavy ram mounted in place of her figurehead came crashing through the sides of the next ship to portside. The long ram struck the next vessel below the waterline, since the prow of the *Thurdan Maid* had fallen low as she rode the swells. Tons of ice-cold water came thundering through the gaping hole rent in her hull and she began to founder.

The Lamp of Madness shone on, swinging on her gimbals with every pitch and toss of the deck. Her beam flashed from ship to ship, bringing murder and madness and riot to each. Five ships she bathed in the Gray Death—a dozen—and yet others.

*

AT the end of his swing through space, Thongor released his grip on the rope and fell crashing to the deck beside the sparkling antenna of the mist machine.

All over the ship the battle sprang to life again now that Belshathla was dead and the Ray of Madness had turned aside to bathe the other vessels in the great armada in its terrible beam.

Barim Redbeard thundered forth his war cry and his great axe clove into the chest of the pirate who stood before him. Thangmar grinned, hefted his huge scimitar, and matched him stroke for stroke. Beyond them the Blue Nomad giant, Roegir, hacked and slew with his mighty broadsword.

Karm Karvus had swung across into the midship deck of the *Red Wolf* and he fought side by side with the roaring pirates of the *Scimitar*. Now he cut his way to the foredeck and climbed up the rail to set his slim

Tsargolian rapier beside the broadsword of the Valkarthan and the Patangan longsword of Charn Thovis.

But his way was opposed by a wild-eyed and half-naked giant brandishing the heft of a broken oar. The burly corsair was in a berserk frenzy and he swung the massive shaft of the oar around his head in terrible whistling strokes. Had one of them connected, it would have hurled Karm Karvus against the rail, broken bones thrusting through mangled flesh. But the Prince dodged beneath the whistling stroke of this terrible club—and, in so doing, he lost his footing in a puddle of wet blood and fell, the blade clattering to the deck from his hand. Grinning, the berserk giant brought his terrible weapon up over his head and whistling down to crush Karm Karvus—

Suddenly a slim boyish figure in tight breeches sprang across the fallen Prince and sent the needle point of a slender rapier flashing for the heaving chest of the giant.

The point slashed through the very heart of the berserk corsair. He stiffened like one struck by lightning, and the club went hurtling overboard from his suddenly strengthless hands. Then he fell slowly, collapsing in a welter of gore. Karm Karvus felt a small strong hand under his arm, and staggered to his feet, to look down into the face of his rescuer.

"Yian!" he gasped.

The Princess of Cadorna laughed up at him with sparkling eyes. He had sternly warned her to remain below decks on the *Scimitar*, but had she obeyed him he might well have feasted before Father Gorm in the Hall of Heroes ere this night had grown much older. So he did not have the heart to chastise her, but simply stood and stared down at her.

Never had she looked more beautiful. The cold wind had whipped fresh color into her cheeks. The black jewels of her almond eyes glittered with mischief. The slim rapier she held clenched in one capable fist was crimson to the hilt, and gave further proof—if further proof were needed—of the truth of her claim that she could ride and hunt and fight like any man.

With her long slender legs clad in the glove-tight breeches, and her loose white blouse stretched taut against the rise of her sharp young breasts, a scarlet kerchief twisted about the heavy black cataract of her hair—she looked very desirable.

He bent and crushed her to him, one arm closing about her slim shoulders, and he kissed her there on the corpse-strewn foredeck of the embattled galley. His lips were fierce and demanding. Her mouth was warm and soft and very sweet.

*

THONGOR turned to smash the mist machine, but the steely glitter of a sabre-blade flickered before him.

He turned to confront Kashtar—at last!

The Red Wolf of Tarakus was very changed. His face was a snarling mask of fury. Red murder blazed in his glaring eyes. His sallow features were slick with sweat and his brow was smeared with hot blood where a sword-point had slashed the flesh. His sleek dark hair was disarranged, and hung wetly in a tangle about his snarling face.

His upper torso was half-naked. Steel had ripped his scarlet raiment to shreds, and his sleek tawny flesh shone wetly with droplets of mist and sweat and gore.

"Dog of a Valkarthan savage!" he spat. "I'll spit your foul heart on the point of my steel!"

"Well, you are welcome to try," Thongor smiled. "You scarlet swine from the garbage heaps of Tarakus," he added.

Their blades met and ere long the silvery clashing music arose. The Valkarthan broadsword is long and heavy and hardly the weapon of choice for dueling. Compared to the steel needle that floated lightly in Kashtar's hand, it was cumbersome and slow. But great thews swelled along Thongor's arm and his thick wrist was strong where sinewy tendons were braided about solid bone. He batted the other's light blade aside, and took a stand.

Kashtar was a master-swordsman, and his steely wrist sent the light point of the rapier flickering. But wherever it danced it rang against the heavy steel of Thongor's blade. Again and again Kashtar sought to find some chink in the web of flying steel that Thongor's broadsword wove in the air between the two of them. Again and again it was struck aside.

His naked chest gleamed as it rose and fell with every panting breath. Sweat stung his eyes and blood from the wound on his brow blurred his vision. Gradually, Kashtar began to weary. The lean muscles in his sword-arm ached with the effort of keeping that narrow blade dancing through the misty air.

It came to Kashtar then that perhaps he could not kill this man.

It was a novel concept, and a little frightening. For never before had the Red Wolf fought one who did not fall before his ravening steel. But, although the effort of fighting thrust needles of red pain through arm and chest and wrist, and although his breath came now in hoarse, ragged panting, and although he employed—one after the other—every trick of swordsmanship he had ever learned . . . he had as yet not even drawn a scarlet scratch across the flesh of his opponent.

Thongor fought silently. His chest rose and fell calmly and he did not seem to weary. Cruel amusement glinted in his strange gold eyes under the scowling black brows, as he read the desperation, the growing fury, and the fear and the frustration in the face of his opponent. Effortlessly he turned aside the flickering blade of Kashtar's sword.

Kashtar began to feel the icy breath of terror.

His face was black with effort now, and he staggered with exhaustion. His heaving chest struggled to suck air into starved lungs. He knew now that Thongor was but playing with him, and this seared him to the very roots of his soul . . . for ever ere now it had been Kashtar who had played the game of cat and mouse . . . and he did not enjoy the reversal of the roles!

Now his eyes flashed and grew narrow with cunning. For his blurred glance had seen a pool of wetness to the left of Thongor's wide-spread feet. And he noted that the Valkarthan's feet were bare. Could he bait Thongor into changing position slightly, then perhaps he could make him slip in that puddle. He began to sidle to his right, drawing Thongor about. Foot by foot in a half-circle he fought, until suddenly the Barbarian lurched and all but lost his balance as his left foot slid in the wetness.

With a hoarse grating laugh, Kashtar drew back his blade—to thrust it deep in Thongor's heart.

But as he swung that needle of steel back it struck an obstacle—

Kashtar's sword touched the copper antenna of the mist machine, which flashed and crackled with its aura of blue fire—*and the Red Wolf of Tarakus stiffened as ten thousand volts of man-made lightning tore through him!*

CHAPTER 18:

TO THE DEATH!

The decks ran red with reeking gore,
The dawn was loud with ringing steel,
Ships broke asunder, till the roar
Of battle made high heaven reel!

—Thongor's Saga, Stave XIX

AS the steel rapier caught and conducted the fury of the electrical force that flowed through the copper antenna, Kashtar's sword glowed ruby red—fiery yellow—then blinding white! Incandescent droplets of smoking metal dribbled down the hilt to his blistered hand.

But Kashtar felt no pain. He was beyond pain now, for the seething fury of the lightning had struck him dead on the instant. Slowly his rigid corpse toppled to the deck and even Thongor bit his lip and turned his eyes away from the thing that had been his face.

The blast of electric fire had left nothing of his features by which he could have been recognized.

Now a sharp explosion sounded within the mechanism. White fire spat viciously from fused electrodes and oily black smoke whirled up from the red-hot coils. The whine of the force field ebbed. No longer did the crackling aura of blue flame sparkle about the copper pole. The primitive Valkarthan knew nothing of electricity—he could not know how or why the steel blade of Kashtar had created a short-circuit that had wrecked the mechanism. He only knew that the mist machine was dead and ruined beyond repair.

And that the Red Wolf of Tarakus would rove the seas no more . . .

About him the battle surged on, but by now Karm Karvus and Yian had gained the foredeck, aye, and Minga and Turan of Barim Redbeard's crew. The five of them, and Charn Thovis swept the foredeck clean of the foe.

Ship after ship of the corsair fleet was turning its prow to investigate the battle that raged in undiminished fury aboard the stricken flagship. The nearer vessels could see that Kashtar's galley had been rammed by another ship, and boat after boat came gliding across the misty waters to investigate, and to lend aid to the Pirate King whose death they could not know.

But young Charn Thovis had beheld the havoc the Lamp of Madness had worked upon many of the nearby vessels. As it swung free on its mounting, the throbbing and colorless ray probing like the burning eye of Avangra the Death God himself, brought madness and terror and red murder to ship after ship.

Now the young chanthar sprang to the controls. He swung the droning tube around and played its flickering gray fire across the nearer of the longboats. Then, as their crews went wild and boat after boat was swamped or overturned beneath the feet of maddened and battling sailors, he turned the probing beam of destruction on the ships that had sent them forth.

In no time, it seemed, half the fleet was thrown into a roiling chaos. Ships swung drunkenly in the hands of raving maniacs, to crash and ram into their neighbors. The orderly lines of the armada broke up in a twinkling, and the fleet lost way and floundered in the choppy waters.

Fires were flaring up on some of the nearer ships, as howling men ran across the decks with blazing torches, setting fire to cordage and canvas and mast. The uproar from the furious battles that seethed on the decks of the nearer vessels turned to shrieks of agony and terror as their rigging burst into a furious blaze. From his place at the death-dealing ray projector, the grim-faced chanthar could see wriggling black figures as scores of men hurled themselves into the dark waves of the Gulf rather than perish amid the roaring holocaust of flames.

His face was pale. His lips were pressed tightly together

and his flesh was drawn. His eyes mirrored the horror of what he saw . . . but he swung the throbbing gray radiance of the humming tube from side to side, bathing ship after ship in the ray.

Sometimes the Gods are just. The horror of death and madness the corsairs would have brought down upon the hapless citizens of the City of the Flame was now turned upon their own heads. He swung the beam back and forth, again and again, until eventually he sickened of the slaughter, and thrust the lever back. Then, even as the humming died and the eerie glow faded and dulled within the sparkling crystal tube, Charn Thovis bent and seized up a fragment of broken oar and battered the Lamp of Madness into a tangle of splintered glass and twisted metal.

The machine from hell should have perished with the fall of elder and God-whelmed Nianga. It should have remained forever hidden from the knowledge of men under the dead dry sands of the Gray Barrens.

But now, at any rate, no man would ever use this horrible invention in war against his fellow men again . . .

He turned away, to join the battle. Then, suddenly, he paused, lifting his head.

"Lord Thongor!" he cried.

The Barbarian turned from his red work. And Charn Thovis did not have to say more. For the clammy fog no longer choked their lungs. Now they breathed in the fresh salt tang of open sea. And, looking up, they saw the faint red glimmer of dawn dim as a ghost of light away to the East.

Kashtar's blade had short-circuited the mist machine and it was dead and cold. And now the clean gusts of wind tore the gray mantle of the fog to ribbons and swept the decks free of its insubstantial tendrils.

Thongor's face broke into a grin of joy. No more the mists of foul enchantment cloaked the invading fleet from watchful eyes. Now the warriors of Patanga would look upon the waters and they would see the cunning and treacherous foe that had crept almost to their gates, and the alarm would go forth. Whether he and his comrades took the *Red Wolf*, or whether they went down at last under the overwhelming numbers of the pirate throng, it no longer mattered. For Patanga was saved . . .

And then the gloomy skies of very early dawn were illuminated by a sudden and almost supernatural explosion of blue-white fire, and Thongor raised his eyes to the open skies above him. And he saw what was there and there was a glory in his face as he looked upon their salvation . . .

*

TOWARDS dawn the senior officer, Changan Jal, wearied of his watch and bade the young Otar, Anzan Varl, to turn the needle-prow of the sleek little airboat back to the soaring pylon of the Air Citadel. His night duty was over and the weary commander looked forward to a cold bottle, warm bed, and a dreamless sleep.

But some slight trace of lurking suspicion concerning that great fogbank he had earlier observed, rolling up the shining waters of the great Gulf in its slow and remorseless advance upon Patanga, came to him even as he spoke the word.

On a sudden impulse he countermanded the order and bade Anzan Varl direct the craft to the waterfront for one last look. Had the immense body of mist dispersed in the winds of early morn? Or would he find the harbor deep under smothering waves of clammy, clinging fog?

Just as the trim little floater arched over the harbor, and as Changan Jal peered down at the roiling mists that had by now moved very close to the sea wall . . . the gusting wind whipped aside the mantle of deception and he saw with a thrill of unearthly shock the black-hulled war galleys of the dread pirates of Tarakus!

Swifter than thought he slapped the throttles home and sent the little craft arrowing down on a long glide. Seizing the controls he swung the gleaming electrode of the sithurl weapon mounted in their prow, until it pointed at the scarlet sails beneath.

No time now to exchange leisurely signals with the watchmen who dwelt in the signal tower atop the crest of the Citadel. Shouting that Anzan Varl should fire at will, to inflict the greatest damage, he sprang from his seat and tore open the locker beneath one of the two bunks built into the little cabin.

From this he snatched up a device the clever hands of the wise Nephelos, Iothondus, had built. By compressed air it fired a rocket which would explode into a blinding flare after a certain period of exposure to the air.

Even as the droning crackle of the lightning gun speared white fire down at the black lean black ships below, Changan Jal sprang to the afterdeck of the floater and fired his signal flare high into the dim air of earliest dawn.

Like a new star burning in the skies of dawn, the flare floated down over the streets and squares of Patanga, a blinding dazzle of blue-white fury.

Never before had the flares been used in earnest. They were only to be employed in moments of ultimate peril. Only in the greatest and most urgent of emergencies were they to blaze in the skies of Patanga.

No sooner had Changan Jal's brilliant flare cast its bright rays above the city, than silvery horns rang out over the spires and towers of the city. A company of the Patangan Archers sprang upon their mounts and went clattering into the streets to man the gates of the city. Airboats broke formation—hovered indecisively for an instant until the thunder of Anzan Varl's sithurl gun drew their attention to the harbor area—then swooped over the waterfront, the dark waves, and the embattled invasion fleet, to join their searing beams to the attacking fire from the lone vessel commanded by Changan Jal.

Like lean and deadly hawks they swooped down upon the confusion of tangled and blazing ships, and like hawks they struck to kill. Soon the darkness before full dawn was ablaze with flickering fingers of fire, and ship after ship exploded into a cloud of flaming wreckage as the stored energy of the sithurl crystals was expended in irresistible beams of electric fire.

*

IT was characteristic of Thongor that, in his delight at the attack of his Air Guard, he did not think of his own peril.

Indeed, it was not until a probing finger of white flame struck the afterdeck of the *Red Wolf* that he realized the circling airboats could not tell friend from foe.

The deck jumped and slapped the soles of his feet as the rear of the ship blew apart in a deafening explosion and an eye-searing flash of white and crimson flame.

Thundering a command to the others who fought with him to hold the foredeck, Thongor sprang lightly over the rail and wove through the staggering throng of battling seamen. The air was thick with oily black smoke now; the upper works were ablaze, and smoking cinders drifted down like some grim Pompeiian rain to bestrew the decks with smoldering sparks.

Seizing the shoulder of Barim Redbeard, Thongor shouted into his ear, striving to make himself heard through the din.

Barim heard, and lifted a golden horn that hung at his waist. Settling it to his lips he blew the call that signaled *return to the ship* to every seaman of the *Scimitar* who still lived on the gory decks of the flagship.

Disengaging from their opponents, the well-trained fighting men of the Redbeard turned almost on the instant and went swinging across the wreckage of the rail to the decks of their own vessel.

Thongor, Karm Karvus and Captain Redbeard were the last men to quit the decks of the burning wreck. The instant his booted feet bestrode the decks of his own ship, Redbeard bellowed to his helmsman to take her out. Seamen snatched up oars and boating hooks and thrust against the broken timbers of the *Red Wolf's* hull, prying their ram loose from the doomed vessel. And not a moment too soon.

For the beam of destruction that had flashed from the hovering airboat had torn a gaping hole in the hull of the *Red Wolf,* and tons of black water were pouring into her hold. Her rigging aflame, her decks strewn with the dead and the dying, the erstwhile flagship of a once-invisible armada was settling visibly. Ere many minutes past she would carry the last of her crew down to a watery grave . . .

But now the *Scimitar* herself was in deadly peril from the airboats that swooped and circled and struck in the skies above. Barim bawled an order that sent fat, puffing Blay across the deck to the lockers, from whence he drew the white flag of surrender. Swift hands tied it to a line and hauled it up into the top mast, replacing the black banner of piracy. Then Redbeard sent his galley curving away to starboard, and soon clear water seperated them from the chaos of burning, sinking, or fleeing ships.

As the *Scimitar* drew in to anchor in the harbor, a company of the City Guard came clattering down the stone quay on racing kroters to disarm the men of the surrendering ship. To their blank astonishment they were met at the rail by Thongor himself. They threw themselves out of the saddle to kneel before the Lord of Patanga, but already he had turned away and his attentions were fixed on the last moments of the doomed fleet.

Half of the armada was sunk, or sinking, or aflame. Many other ships wandered unscathed, but their erratic course suggested that their decks had been bathed in the throbbing radiance of the Lamp of Madness, and their crew were now a band of howling madmen.

Some of the vessels in the rear ranks turned to flee. But the Air Guards of Patanga were striking for the kill, and they mercilessly tracked down and blew to flaming ruin each of the fleeing galleys.

Few, very few, of the pirate ships surrendered, and thus escaped the holocaust that raged there in the great Battle of the Patanga Gulf.

By far the greater portion of the fleet were destroyed. Nearly one hundred ships went to a flaming death in this battle, and the loss of human life was in the thousands.

But as the first rays of dawn touched to rose and gold the tallest of the towers of Patanga, the Battle was ended.

And Patanga was saved.

CHAPTER 19:

KINGS OF THE WEST

A word given,
A friend made.
A friendship tested,
A world saved.

—The Scarlet Edda

IT was the better part of a month later, in the early days of Amgor, the first month of winter.

Although chill and gusty winds blew down from the mountains of the North and frost had withered the few remaining leaves to scarlet and gold, the Sun of noon blazed brilliantly in a clear azure sky and it would be long before the coming of Kyramon the Month of Snows rendered the season intolerable.

A great procession moved through the streets of Patanga, beginning on the steps of the mighty Temple of the Nineteen Gods, circling once the Great Plaza at the city's heart, and then rolling forth into that splendid avenue that was known as the Thorian Way.

At the fore rode heralds in the black and flamy gold of royal Patanga, and yet others in the scarlet of Tsargol, the green of Tarakus, and the pale gold of westernmost Cadorna by the sea.

Then came a troop of the Patangan Archers, their nimble kroters glittering in jeweled harnesses. The archers wore dress helmets of sparkling gold; gems flashed from cherm and cuirass and girdle; tall gold plumes nodded from the crest of their shining helms. At their head rode Prince Dru, the cousin of Sumia, Thongor's queen; as hereditary Daotar of the Patangan Archers, he led them at the fore of the mighty pageant.

Behind the bowmen a cohort of the Black Dragons strode on foot, and their gray and grizzled commander,

Zad Komis, marched at their head. Black cloaks swung from the broad shoulders of the grim warriors, and the bright sunlight flashed from the dragon helms they wore, and glittered on the jeweled hilts of their mighty broadswords.

Following this came a bridal chariot drawn by a snow-white zamph, its great wheels rumbling over the smooth flagstones. In this chariot Karm Karvus and his young bride, Yian of Cadorna, rode. The Lord of Tsargol lifted a hand to acknowledge the plaudits of the throng gathered to watch the procession. But his other arm was about the shoulders of the lovely girl who had become his queen but moments before, as they stood together at the foot of the great altar.

Then came the Lord of the West himself, in a mighty chariot drawn by two lumbering zamphs, the war standard of imperial Patanga going before. Splendid in kingly robes, his radiant queen beside him. Thongor smiled as the crowd thundered forth his name. With him in the chariot of state rode his young son, Prince Thar, and the Prince Kazan, Lord of Cadorna, father of Yian, smiling on the cheering throng.

Chariot after chariot followed that of the Lord of the West, and in them rode the barons and princes, the lords and nobles, the courtiers and officials of the Empire. In one of these, looking distinctly uncomfortable in his stately robes, was Barim Redbeard. His blazing bush of whiskers was newly trimmed; gone were his usual gaudy kerchief, baldric, sea-boots and axe. He rode this day in the green velvet royal robes of Tarakus, and the emerald-and-silver diadem of that city glittered about his brows. Wrapped in the long robes, holding the trident sceptre in one awkward hand, the Redbeard was flushed and stiff. But he carried himself with dignity, as became a new king. For not a half an hour before, on the steps of the altar, Thongor had proclaimed him as Lord of Tarakus. And he had knelt there before the Black Hawk and accepted him as his overlord and emperor, and thus the staunch and hearty old seaman became one of the Kings of the West and a seventh city was added to the Empire of Thongor the Mighty.

The days just past lingered in the thoughts of Barim of Tarakus as he rode through the splendid streets of Patanga. After the alert Changan Jal had discovered the presence of the fleet and given the alarm, the Air Guard had broken the pirate fleet and burned or sunk or captured every last ship that had sailed therein. In the busy days that had followed, the flying legions of Patanga had carried war to the gates of Tarakus itself, and after some street battles and a few days of siege, the men who held the Pirate City had surrendered before the irresistible might of the City of the Flame. It was well-done. All but impregnable at the end of its lone promontory, walled about with the bastion of the sea, the fortress-like city might have held out longer for a grueling siege—for, although his sky navy could have shattered the walls of Tarakus and swept its streets and houses with devastion, Thongor held his airboats in check for he had no wish to turn the city into a flaming ruin.

But few men were left to man the walls of the Pirate City, as Kashtar Red Wolf had taken most of the fighting men with him to the conquest of Patanga. Those who were left behind were either old seamen unfit for the hardships of battle, or peaceful tradesmen, inn-keepers, cobblers and the like, or those who had for one or another reason earned tne enmity of the Red Wolf of Tarakus and had been languishing in his dungeons. These had no heart for battle, and no cause, now that the armada was destroyed and both Kashtar and his grim accomplice, Belshathla, were slain. Hence, after some little show of resistance, cooler heads prevailed and the gates were opened to the legions of Thongor.

As well, more peaceful expeditions had consumed the days just past. A princely flagship of the aerial navy had flown to distant Cadorna, over the waters of the Gulf and the trackless jungles of Kovia, to bring the Princess Yian home to the city of her fathers. On this glad voyage she had been accompanied by her gallant rescuer, Karm Karvus. The Lord of Tsargol had a double mission in this venture; not only did he serve to escort the Princess to safety, but he came to sue for her hand in marriage. The dignified, elderly Lord Kazan of Cadorna was delighted and relieved to see his long lost daughter alive and well, for he had long since given her up for dead, assuming her pleasure boat to have been lost at sea. And once he had taken her into his fatherly embrace, and heard an account of her adventures and how the brave young Prince of Tsargol had saved her from amidst the very stronghold of the corsairs, he gladly gave his paternal consent.

While these thoughts had been passing through the memories of Prince Barim, the mighty procession had advanced down the Thorian Way and they were now before the gates of the Palace of Patanga. Here they dismounted and made their entrance.

*

THE hall of the Hundred Kings had not changed from the way it had been many weeks ago when last Barim Redbeard had seen it. Still the great circle of stone faces gazed down upon the dais of the throne from the base of the mighty dome. Sunlight streamed gloriously through tall narrow windows of many-colored glass, casting glowing color across the noble throng gathered there before the Flame Throne to see the Lord Thongor dispense honors and ennoblement to those who had earned such in the perilous days just past.

Gules and emerald, azure and topaz, purple and gold, the colors lay across the glistening stone pave and flashed from sword-hilt and gemmy coronet.

For this occasion, the thrones of the Sarkaja and the Jasark were drawn up to either side of the central throne.

When his wife and son had taken their places on the dais, and all the brilliant assemblage was arranged to the satisfaction of Pheris Marn and Zaldon Thald, the Chamberlain and the Chancellor, Thongor strode up the central aisle past bowing men and women. Up the nine steps of the dais of black marble he strode, and to the foot of the Flame Throne itself, while the Lord Chancellor rang his great silver mace of office against the polished tiles, and cried out in a deep voice—

"Hai, Sarkon! Hail, Great King! All ye that stand here, let ye know that ye are in the Presence of the Great

Prince Thongor the Mighty, the King of Patanga, the Emperor of the Seven Cities. And let all hail the Lord of the West . . ."

And ere the solemn echoes of his stately proclamation could die, a great cry came from a hundred throats.

"Hail to the Lord of the West!"

Standing before the Flame Throne, the hilt of Sarkozan under his hand, Thongor looked down upon his people. Splendid and kingly was he as he stood there, robed in the black imperial velvet with the Gold Shield of Patanga upon his breast, charged with the Black Hawk of Valkarth.

From the dimness of the shadowy dome above him a vagrant beam of sunlight fell, striking to flashing fire the Flame Crown that sat his brow, all of pure redgold and studded with sparkling chandrals. Bleak and grim and impassive was the bronze mask of his features, but those that knew him well could read the glint of satisfaction in his eye, the deep happiness in the slight smile that touched his lips, and the pride in his tall stance.

His eyes swept the hall to either side of the dais, where a half-circle of thrones had been drawn up, facing the throng. Therein seated, the shield of their domain above their heads, sat the Princes Zul of Zangabal, Turmis of Shembis, Thon of Thurdis, Karvus of Tsargol, Thal of Pelorm, and Barim of Tarakus.

He began speaking without preamble.

"Long have I desired to give honor to this man for his many services to the realm and to my house. Let him come forward now and receive his reward, and my gratitude."

The silver mace rang on the marble floor and the deep voice of the Chancellor rang out—

"Charn Thovis of Vozashpa, *kojan* of the Empire and leader of the Ninth Cohort of the Black Dragons, come forth!"

His face pale, his shoulders back, as erect as if he stood on parade, the young chanthar stepped before the dais of the Flame Throne and met the approving eyes of his Lord as Thongor smiled on him from above.

"For three years now the barony of Tallan has lain vacant since the hand of the Jasark my son struck down Dalendus Vool when he sought to usurp my station. Kneel, Charn Thovis, and rise as the Lord of Tallan!"

Flushed with pleasure, the stalwart young warrior received from Thongor's hand the coronet of his lordship. Bowing to the smiles of Princess Sumia, and receiving a boyish grin and a mischievous wink from Prince Thar, the new Lord of Tallan returned to his place at the forefront of the throng.

Thongor was again speaking.

"In a very large degree, the freedom of Patanga on this happy day is the work of the alertness and the vigilance of one brave officer, and we are all in his debt. Let this man step forward now."

Again the ring of the great mace against stone, and the sonorous voice of Zaldon Thald sounded through the length of the hall.

"Changan Jal of Patanga, senior Daotar of the Air Guard, come forth!"

His winged silver helm flashing in the sunlight, his cloak of sky-blue silk fluttering from his lean shoulders, resplendent in the metallic silver harness of the air navy, the graying officer who had first seen the invasion fleet, first to flash the alarm that woke the city to arms, and first to strike at the ships of Tarakus, strode proudly to the foot of the dais.

"Kneel, Changan Jal, Daotar, and rise as Vice-Daotarkon of the Air Guard and a *kojan* of the Empire!"

The bestowal of honors now done, the Chancellor led the throng in a thunderous acclaim for the Lords of the West there assembled. And when the Hall of the Hundred Kings was silent once more, Thongor smiled and said:

"And now let us all go in to dinner!"

*

AND here my story ends—as all good stories should—with a victory, a wedding, and a feast.

". . . Even the Pirates of Tarakus, armed with the dread power of the Gray Magicians of elder time, could not stand against the Warrior of Valkarth, and fell before him, and thus the seventh city of the West came beneath the Black Hawk Banner, and thus the Golden Empire grew from year to year."

So it is written in the third chapter of the Fifth Book of The Lemurian Chronicles.

APPENDIX:

THE AEON OF THE GRAY MAGICIANS

THOSE passages from *The Lemurian Chronicles* which record the lost history of the Gray Magicians of Nianga, and to which the Hierarch Eodrym refers in the third chapter of this novel, are among the few fragments of that mighty volume which have survived the ages into our own day. I thought it might amuse my readers to see the actual text to which Eodrym alludes.

The Lemurian Chronicles were written down half a million years ago. The tongue wherein this ancient lore was recorded has perished from human knowledge; the very continent whereon these words were written down has foundered beneath the waves; but a few scraps of the age-old book survive where all else is forgotten.

But here is a page from that lost book.

From THE THIRD BOOK:

ii. The Nine Cities of the West Are Founded

. . . Thus it came to pass that the Children of Nemedis passed thither into the West and they builded in those lands the Nine Cities of Thurdis and Kathool, Cadorna, Zangabal and Shembis, Tsargol and Tarakus and Pelorm, and Patanga the City of the Flame. And there they rested and begat tall sons and fair daughters, and three thousand years of time went by.

iii. The Era of the Gray Magicians

But eastwards in the land of Nianga dark forces were at work. For there had risen up in those lands, over the centuries since the Fall of Nemedis and the coming-hence of men into the West, a mighty Kingdom whereof there were three great cities of Kuth and Shandathar and grim Zanjan. And the black wizards of remotest Zaar, leagued with the cunning Serpent in his secret isles amidst the Inner Sea, went amongst this folk and won them to evil ways with the promise of power. And thus arose the reign of the Gray Magicians, as men did call them with fear and trembling.

iv. Gray Magic

Of old was it set down in the mighty pages of the Scarlet Edda that the Magicians of Nianga didst seek to seize and tame even the Ultimate Fires of Our Lord the Sun himself; and that they hadst won the mastery of a great art whereby men might wield forces so vast that the mighty Earth itself couldst be shaken forth from its sphere amidst the firmament of heaven, and that the dry land and the great sea shouldst both be consumed in a torrent of ever-burning flame, should ever these Forces break free from their control.

v. The Doom of Nianga

Yet ere the Gray Magicians had set their hand upon the delicate balance of forces whereof is the Earth maintained among the spheres and the fires of the mighty Sun held in balance, a vast and shadowy Doom fell over these lands, and the cities of Kuth and Shandathar and grim Zanjan were overthrown and the people thereof fled. And that land became a desolate wilderness which men called the Gray Barrens, where none do dwell. Some say it was the Gods, but others say the hand of Nature smote them down, they who wouldst tamper with the Laws whereby Creation is held firm amidst Chaos.

vi. The West Riseth.

Thus it was that the Gray Magicians fell who dared toy with those Forces whereof the very stars of the firmament are sustained, each in his appointed sphere and station; thus were they undone by the very powers they sought to control . . .